Time of Grace

Olwyn Harris

Reading Stones Publishing

Dedication:

To the women who have been the voice of Abigail to me,
praying and walking with me through all sorts of times...
especially Gaye.

Redwood Park

1879

Abigail was an intelligent and beautiful woman...
"May you be blessed for your good judgment,
for keeping me from bloodshed,
and from avenging myself with my own hands..."

(1 Samuel 25:3, 33)

I.

"Callie? I wanted to ask... how is Ted doing? How are his wounds?"

Callie picked up the hairbrush and began to brush her mistress' long hair. Their eyes connected in the mirror of the dressing table where Abby sat. "Oh Ma'am. It doesn't seem fair. He wasn't meaning to be disrespectful. But he does get ideas sometimes."

Abby felt her stroke tremble and she reached up and placed a gentle hand over hers. "I know Callie. I know. I just wanted to check he was okay."

Abby watched Callie's face in the mirror of her dressing table. Callie began to blink her eyes quickly as she continued to brush her hair with long strokes. "I wouldn't know Ma'am," she said evasively.

"You don't know? How can you not know? Haven't you been checking on him? You are allowed to tend him."

"Yes Ma'am. I know. It's just... well..."

"It's just what Callie? Oh no. Oh no. Don't tell me... has he...?"

"Oh no Ma'am. Nothing bad, but his back... it still weeps some. It just doesn't seem to be..."

"His wounds are not healing?"

"Oh Ma'am, I spoke wrongly. He is recovering fine, I'm sure of it. It's just that... well, he left."

"He's left you? You've just found out you're pregnant and he's left? Oh Callie. I would never have thought that of him!"

"Oh no, Ma'am! Me and Ted are fine. What I mean is... he's left Mister Bates. He left his employ. He no longer works here."

"But wouldn't you go with him?"

"Oh no Ma'am. I couldn't leave. Not while you're here."

"But Callie, he's your... Why wouldn't you go with him?" she repeated. Abby paused then and nodded. "I thank you though, Callie. I do. I would miss you more than I could say. When will you see him again?"

"Oh, Ma'am not long. Just the day after the morrow... on my next day off. I can see him then."

"Really? But where would he go? Did he get work at the other stations in the valley? I didn't think they would take our men. Sorenson was pretty clear about what he would do if he found others poaching his men."

"No, not there, Ma'am. Even though he tried, none of them would take him. Still, it's not that far. I will see him soon," and the strokes of her brushing quickened again.

"Oh..." A frown puckered her brow, and she shook her head slightly. Callie was talking in riddles, and it didn't make sense. "As long as he's okay."

"I believe he is Ma'am. More okay than he's been for a long time. He's got help tending his back."

"Well, that is good. And you? Are you okay?"

"Yes Ma'am. If you are here, and you are doing well... I am in the right place."

She smiled slightly. Doing well? She was not sure about that. But getting through. She stood up and Callie helped her into her nightgown. Abby was thoughtful and then paused, something dawning on her.

"Callie?"

"Yes Ma'am..."

"Those rumours of bushrangers... that disgraced lawyer..."

Callie turned away and began to busily tidy the dressing table, picking up hair-pins and putting them in a bowl. Abby lifted the lamp and put it on the side table. She went over to her and lowered her voice. "Did he join them? Is that why he is not far away? Have they moved onto our land? Sorensen would never allow it."

"Oh no Ma'am. They are up in the hills, past the boundary. Ted told me that the bushland there is non-gazetted Crownlands. They are not breaking any laws being there."

"Along the Gilyard Range? Up there?"

"I don't know for sure Ma'am. They are not supposed to say," she said quickly, retracting her lapse in caution.

"Oh..." She went over to a carafe of water and poured herself a drink. "Callie, when is your next day off?"

"Day after the morrow Ma'am. Just the same as always. This week is my turn."

"Well, tomorrow I will help you put together a kit: bandages, salve, oil... that sort of thing. Take those things to help tend his wounds." She paused and then added, "... and put in some extra buns, those ones with the seeds that Ted likes."

"Cook's bread-buns, Ma'am? Really?"

"I remember you said he likes them. We would never offer benefit to a band of fugitives, but it would be entirely appropriate for you to take bread to your husband. How hungry do you think he would be... since he was hurt so badly?"

"Ahh Ma'am. Um. Pretty hungry... I guess?" She didn't say Ted had lost his appetite, and his wounds were now seeping with pus.

"And how hungry would that be? Eight... ten... a dozen rolls? Would that be enough?"

"Oh! Maybe fifteen Ma'am. He is pretty hungry."

"Well... that is hungry. Sorensen is back this weekend, and since he is bringing some associates with him, it is entirely reasonable that we will over-cater. A few rolls will not be missed. Let's double it... take thirty. I'll cover it with Cook. Please Callie, don't tell anyone where you suspect Ted has gone. It is safer that way."

"Yes Ma'am. Thank you, Ma'am. Anything else before you retire?"

"No, thank you Callie. I will be fine. Please... be watchful."

"Yes Ma'am. Good night."

Oh yes, tonight was a good night. After all, Sorensen was away.

2

Callie put Abby's early morning tea tray on her bed and opened the curtains. Abby sat up and stretched with a look of determination.

"Callie? You know you don't have to bring in my tray on your day off. But since you are here, I have news. I am decided. I will come with you. I want to see for myself that Ted's wounds are healing satisfactorily."

"But Ma'am!"

"This happened while he was in our employ. The least I can do is to try to sort some kind of restitution. Even so, I know it is hardly enough."

"Ma'am it was not your fault. You tried to stop it."

"I'm certain that a horse-riding excursion is completely advantageous to my constitution. You will be accompanying me. No one need be privy to the details of our outing."

Callie looked away. There was a code of loyalty to Mistress Abby at the homestead. She doubted any would betray her even if they knew.

They rode the horses along the track that led to the old dump out by the eastern boundary. It was a barren, rocky sort of place in the foothills that was no good for pasture. There was a collection of broken dray wheels, bed frames, pipes, barrels, and an assortment of other non-combustible refuse.

"Ma'am, Ted told me this is the place. I am sorry it is such a common sort of place to meet, but he said it had to be." She went to a particular barrel and lifted out a fragment of mirror. She glinted it in the sunlight on the trees lining the boundary. "We tether our horses here Ma'am in the shade... and we wait."

"I thought you would take me straight there. How long will we have to wait?"

"I don't know Ma'am. Ted never said. But he said I had to be patient. I bought a book for you to read."

"A book? Oh." Abby shook her head. The subterfuge was quite intriguing. But then, Ted had sought refuge with a man who had a price on his head, a private bounty as incentive for information. When she heard about it, Abby was not surprised the firm published the reward to cover the embarrassment. She sat down near the horses in the shade and opened her book.

"Ma'am, I brought a snack as well, if you are inclined."

"No. I'm fine, thanks." She glanced towards the line of thick trees and tried to distinguish any movement. There was nothing. She soon resigned herself to the distraction of her book and continued reading.

She jolted as a shadow passed over the page. She looked up into the rough faces of two men. She glanced over at Callie who sat very still, drained of all colour. Abby closed her book gently and slowly stood up. She nodded. "Good morning, gentlemen," she said benignly.

They frowned. "Are you Blue's missus?"

"Blue?"

"You know. Ted... Ted Horne, Blue."

"Oh. Well, no, not me. That would be Callie here."

"Then why are *you* here?"

"I am a concerned friend. I want to see that Mr Horne's wounds are healing satisfactorily."

"Mister huh?" They scoffed. "Lady, we are living in the scrub, barely able to scrape up the basics to stay alive. 'Mister' is not required here. If we get by, we think that is satisfactory enough."

"I have brought some things that may help with healing his wounds. I have done nursing. There is no need to delay."

They looked at each other confused. "I dunno. It was only supposed to be Blue's girl."

"Oh, come gentlemen. You can hardly suppose I seem like a threat? I have brought a kit, and Callie has some personal things for Ted. And we have fresh bread rolls that might make for a pleasant lunch today." She went to the horses and passed them some calico flour bags. "Try to carry these bags without crushing them."

One man roughly opened the bag and then took a glorious long whiff of the freshly baked bread. "Damn! This is like manna from Heaven! I'm reckoning the Capt'n won't mind." He grabbed a bun and threw another to his mate. "Hawk, this is a damned sight better than your cooking. It's just like she said... what threat could a slip of yarn like her be?"

His companion shrugged as he ripped it open with his teeth and took a bite. "I reckon, it sure wouldn't hurt Blue to have some proper help rather than your heavy hand," Hawk said, building their case. "Up to you to cover it with Red though."

Abby raised her fine eyebrows as she listened to their banter, mildly amused.

He turned to Abby and shrugged. "We'll have to blindfold you."

"Blindfold? Really gentlemen, we come in peace."

"Rules be rules."

She took a deep breath. "Very well. We will do our best not to attack you with our charm."

"See Dickens. This is what you need: a bit of charm. You could take lessons," Hawk said with a smirk.

"I is Prince Charming me-self," Dickens grunted as he produced a grubby tattered piece of rag from his shabby vest pocket.

Abby held up her hand and then removed her scarf. "I would prefer to use this... if you don't mind? Does this meet the requirements of your rules?"

"Does okay I guess."

She nodded and applied the folded scarf over her eyes. They left their horses and were led by foot over the uneven ground. She stumbled on the rough rocks under her boots and gripped her guide tightly as she was led forward. Then they stopped. She could hear the gentle whinny of a horse. "We ride from here." She could hear Callie being hoisted up behind a saddle also. They clung onto their riders as they went higher, up and up into the mountains.

Eventually they stopped. Some rough hands lifted her down and as Abby went to remove her scarf, someone held her wrist firmly, restraining her. He spoke. "Mrs Horne, your husband is over there. Hawk will show you."

Abby heard running; Callie crying; Ted speaking, reassuring her he was okay. The last time she saw Ted he was at the point of collapse. At least he was strong enough to talk now. That gave her hope.

❧

3.

The one holding her wrist spoke again. "Dickens! What is she doing here?"

"She came with Blue's missus. We couldn't just leave her there."

"Why not?"

"She bought us bread."

"You were bribed with a loaf of bread?"

"Buns... enough for all of us. She ain't no threat. She said she had skills... you know... abilities... to tend Blue's back."

His voice slowed. "And if I told you I was the Queen's Mother, and you were now the Duke of York, it doesn't necessarily make it so. Take her to my quarters. Leave the blindfold on. She is not to see any location-markers."

Abby turned to the voice. "I didn't come to see *you*. I came only to see Mr Horne."

"Well Ted, at this moment, is with his wife. You can meet him later... if... and only *if*... that is agreeable to him." He still held her while her wrists were being bound firmly with some rag, presumably in lieu of available rope.

"Is this really necessary? I believe I came here voluntarily."

"Dickens take her across! I'll be over in a bit."

"Wait!" exclaimed Abby, but suddenly Dickens was entirely inflexible. Her cajoling fell on deaf ears as he resolutely led her away. He sat her down on a rough sort of stump. "This is ridiculous! I have only come to check how Mr... how Ted... Blue... is doing, because Callie said his back was still weeping. After this amount of time, that does not sound good to me so I brought a kit that may help in the tending of his wounds." She continued for a while in a defensive monologue: justifying her presence, her qualifications to offer such a service and the obstruction of goodwill that had been a constant trial her entire life. She slowed her tirade as she increasingly became aware of the silence. "Hello!" Nothing. "Hello?" More silence.

"Are you done?"

"Oh." She swallowed. "Yes sir."

"Are you sure? Because I really don't have the time to listen to more unimpressive justifications of your bizarre behaviour just now."

She inhaled quickly and thought of a million things she wanted to say in response! She took another deep breath. "I am sure."

"Okay. So, tell me. Who are you?"

"Could you take the blindfold off? Please."

"Well. Since you asked nicely." She could feel him behind her, and he loosened her scarf. He dropped it in her lap carelessly. He left her wrists bound.

Abby blinked and opened her eyes. She was seated facing the wall... if it could be called a wall. It was a very primitive sort of structure made of woven twigs and brush. She pivoted around and looked about the room slowly. It was a cave, which went back into the mountainside. A lamp flickered on the desk. The man was seated on a small stool that matched his eclectic collection of improvised furniture pieces, probably constructed from junk salvaged from their tip.

She sat there and considered this man whose reputation had stirred her curiosity. He had dark hair and beard. His serious green eyes were studying the subject before him, unperturbed by her silent observation. He was dressed tidily enough, but obviously lacked access to a good laundry or seamstress.

"Good morning, Sir. You asked who I am. My name is Mrs Abigail Bates."

"Hmm. Missus Bates. Of Redwood Park. It is rather bad manners, even for someone of your position, to come visiting uninvited."

"Sir! No one has ever accused me of ill-manners before."

"Is that because they didn't have the courage to challenge your pretty face, or is this the first time you have conducted yourself in such an uncouth manner?"

"Augh! Uncouth! I think it is not me who is behaving improperly!"

"What does your husband think of you visiting the riffraff up in the hills? Or did he commission you to spy on us?"

She swallowed. "Oh..."

"Oh?" He raised his dark brow and waited.

"Well... as it happens, Mr Bates is currently away. In town on business. I made this decision on my own. He doesn't know I am here, and I probably won't tell him. It will be easier if I don't."

"Hmm: a wife with an independent and subversive streak. Rude *and* rebellious. Is that why you were keen to bother the lair of this notorious outlaw? Were you hoping to find some accommodation?"

"Ohh!" In her outrage she flashed him a heated look of disgust. His serious eyes were laughing at her. She calmed and allowed a smile to flutter around her lips. He was playing with her, like a cat plays with a mouse... just before he eats it. She had to show a little sense, because she quickly realised the flattery of social smiles-and-wiles would be ineffective here. This was not what she expected. "Well, I was curious to be sure. But I assure you; I was quite genuine when I said I was concerned for Ted's wellbeing. He was hurt very badly."

"So, you can beat a man within an inch of his life; leave him to rot in a ditch, and then drop by a couple of weeks later to see if he made it? It doesn't sound very concerned to me."

Abby paled. She went to say something. And then closed her mouth again and sat quietly watching him.

"So, you have nothing to say in the defence of that inexcusable position? The evidence is not looking respectable for you, Mrs Bates, even if you come sporting a respectable wardrobe."

"You are right. It is an appalling situation. I have nothing to say... except that..."

"Ahh. And there it is. The justification of the positioned self-righteous who cannot help but to rationalise inhumanity."

"But I did try a number of times to find how he was and what he might need. I offered what I could, but everyone was so tight lipped. I now know why."

"You now know... what?"

"Well, because he came to you of course. But I didn't know that then. It was only when Sorenson was away, and Callie was by herself, that I was able to get her to talk to me."

"Hmm."

"Sir, I am sorry if I have offended your sensibilities by coming here. In all seriousness, I thought it was a way to start righting a wrong."

"You accuse me of sensibilities? I hardly think our position is that delicate. We are living as exiles in the face of unthinkable injustice. Every man here has his story. Your Ted included. You are insulting the reality of our dire circumstances, Mrs Bates."

"Forgive me. I never intended to insult."

He considered her for a bit, and then stood up abruptly. "Very well. Forgiveness is extended. But you need to understand the tenuous nature of our position. You cannot come here. We have acquired a level of stability in these hills. I cannot allow anyone to jeopardise this, no matter how tormented they are by their culpability."

"You are a hard man, Sir."

He extended his hand in a gesture. "Ruben Davey."

Abby tilted her head. "Well, Mr Davey, your reputation is widely circulated. However, I think the stories are a little more colourful than reality."

"Have I disappointed your expectations for entertainment, Mrs Bates?"

"Not at all. Although I am surprised you have allowed me to see your face, and that you have given me your name."

"Were you expecting my name to be more melodramatic? Something in the manner of Captain Thunderbolt? Which I admit is a tone more interesting than Fred Ward. Or Captain Moonlite? Midnight? Starlight? It seems those of us who have chosen to live outside the respectability of society have a propensity for theatrical pseudonyms, with a particular inclination for nocturnal weather." He shrugged. "It seems I lack the creativity for clever nametags. Some of my men call me 'Captain Red', although personally, I think that utterly lacks imagination."

"Why Red?"

"Why is Ted named Blue when he has red hair? I don't think logic is necessarily part of the equation. Perhaps it stuck because Blackbeard has been used."

She tilted her head and offered a wisp of a smile. "You have no need to embellish your image, Mr Davey. Like I said, your reputation goes before you."

"Yet you still accuse me of dramatizing for effect. Well, the reality is, I don't like to talk about myself."

"But that court case? The 'Inland Ambush' case? No one ever thought the sentencing would go that way. It was a victory that was greatly celebrated in some quarters and caused a great deal of controversy in others."

"Just goes to show, controversy can be one's undoing."

She stood, went over to him and lifted her wrists for him to untie them. "I will respect your wishes, Mr Davey. I will not traverse your hospitality again. Thank you for what you are doing for Ted. If I could see him before I go, I would appreciate it."

He took the scarf she held in her bound hands and ignored the implication to untie her wrists. "The blindfold goes back on when you are outside. You can then legitimately say you have no idea where our camp is."

"Be reassured, Mr Davey, I would not give that information even if I had it."

"Let's not test that theory, shall we? There are ways to extract information."

Dickens led her over to a small, enclosed lean-to that made use of an overhanging outcrop of rock as the ceiling. He unbound her hands, led her inside and then lifted her blindfold. Callie was gently tending Ted, tears rolling down her face as she tried to swab the pus that was weeping from scabbing wounds across his back. Abby gaped at the state of his lacerations. His skin was angry, pus crusted where the lashes had broken his skin, flies buzzed around his back. She turned to Dickens abruptly. "Take me back to Mr Davey. Now!"

"Yes Ma'am," he said, and she decisively followed him back to his walled cave. Dickens had barely pulled aside the canvas curtain before she barged in.

Davey was working at his table and looked up with a raised brow. "I generally do not take visitors, and yet here you are – uninvited – twice in one morning."

She went to say something and then took a deep breath and calmed herself, her lips firm and tight.

He put down his pen and turned to her. "So, are you satisfied? Ted Horne is alive and now you are ready to retire to the sanctity of your lavishly comfortable drawing-room. That didn't take long."

"No, I am not satisfied! Do you not have access to water here?"

He tilted his head and his brow creased, interest stirring in his green eyes. "We live in caves. What do you think?"

"If I knew the answer, Mr Davey, it would be superfluous for me to ask. Do you have access to clean water?" she repeated.

"Enough of it. There are some natural reservoirs along the range. A permanent creek out further."

"Is there sufficient to make a bath?"

"Really? This is about personal toilet? The men will not be tamed to your social sense of grooming. Not many of them will even use a shaving strap and razor. Myself included."

She looked confused, and then almost laughed at his absurd take on her concerns. "Now who is accusing who of sensibilities? I am not here for social reform, Mr Davey. If you and your men want to live like uncivilised cavemen, who am I to judge? I am here because Ted's back is not healing as it should. He needs to have salt baths, in the manner of the convict ships and the prison wards."

"You want to perpetuate his punishment? I don't think so."

"You are a learned man, Mr Davey. Salt baths may be harsh, but they help heal the wounds. The broken skin is weeping with pus. Have you not inspected these wounds yourself?"

"Dickens was checking on him."

"Dickens does not have your learning. The baths will help. You can forgo scrubbing the wounds with bristled brooms, but they do need to be washed with some sort of clean cloth. If you don't have the means of bathing in a tub, a bowl of salted water could suffice."

"You are serious about this. Does he really need it?"

"Yes, it is *needful*. He can't do it himself. I'll get you some salt. Put a generous amount in the water that is used to wash his back. Use the salve once a day and it needs to be cleaned off again every day with the fresh salt bath. I will send back some clean sheets for bandages as well. They are not for sleeping in. Bandages only – to cover the area. Burn the soiled ones when they are taken off. This needs to be done every day – without exception."

❦

4.

Sorenson stared expansively around the dining room of Redwood Park homestead. There were so many prominent faces, powerful men and wealthy wallets sitting at his table; eating his food; drinking his wine; smiling at his maids. Sheep-station was its own class of society, even though they had their fair share of town life. However, Sorensen noticed his wife increasingly preferred to stay out here. That being the case, he would bring society to Redwood Park. They needed to see his healthy tracts of land, his fashionable homestead, his well-bred sheep and quality stock horses, his full complement of station-hands, and... of course... his wife whom other men envied. Beauty like hers was a remarkable commodity in this influential lifestyle.

Abby sat through the soup, attempting to contribute to some level of congenial conversation. The topics discussed rarely varied, regardless of whether the men were in town, at the club, or around a dining table on a sheep-station. The enduring point of interest at the moment was the spat of sheep duffing incidents. Stock had been lost right across the valley, and out onto the plains.

Sorensen raised his glass and scoffed. "Gentlemen. You need to manage your places and your men. I have not had one misplaced ram, wether, or ewe. Not one! Take from my example: A firm hand sends a firm message." The inventory in his head became longer. He was a self-made man. He was the embodiment of success. This is what the young pups around the table aspired to. This is what the old veterans resented. This is what his peers respected.

Abby sat through the main course with a polite smile. She sat through dessert with a bilious feeling sitting in her stomach. After the meal proper, she tried to excuse herself a number of times, but Sorensen refused to release her. She knew she had to sit on the mantelpiece a little longer. So, she smiled and tried to swallow the reflux in her mouth, rinsing it down every so often with a little sugared water. She had Cook make up a concoction of water coloured to the right shade of red wine so that she could out-drink and out-toast all at the table without ever getting to the embarrassing inebriated state of everyone else. This was part of her responsibility as a showcase trophy. Always sober, always smiling, always amiable.

Sorensen stumbled to his feet and made an extravagant toast, general and vague – to the wellbeing of all that is respectable and grand in life! She raised her glass. "Respectable and grand." Yet the picture in her mind was not the opulence and excesses before her, but a dusty little cavern in the hills, the occupant with serious green eyes sitting at a table made from the cast-off rim of a wagon wheel. And she smiled as a scripture flowed through her mind: '*Better is the poor that walketh in his uprightness, than a rich man who is perverse in his ways.*' Better indeed!

Sorensen saw her smile and gloated over the completeness of his circumstances. The ladies around the table giggled and flirted with their dining companions and envied the situation of their hostess.

⁕⁕⁕

Redwood Park had a custom of lavish hospitality for visitors. The entire top floor was dedicated to guest rooms, and the maids were running up and down the stairs to attend to their needs all day. In the mornings, the men would ride around the station, enjoy the outdoors, do a little shooting, talk a little business, while Abby would host a High Tea. The ladies would sip tea, and nibble delicacies while overlooking the garden from the top verandah. The women, particularly, anticipated this opportunity to gossip aside from the prying ears of their husbands. Abby poured the tea and passed around delicate China patterned plates. Her guests politely oohed and aahed at the scrumptious treats and scrutinised the intricate designs on their cups.

Abby kept a list of generally benign conversation topics at her disposal: the best Manchester linen; the finest fashion houses; the latest design in crinolines; the prettiest flowers in bloom; the tastiest ways to serve quail. But inevitably, the topics favoured were the latest scandalous tragedies to befall the nicest of folk. But where Abby would normally divert such a topic of conversation back to the realms of safety, this time she hesitated.

Francine Moore put down her cup. "Did you hear the latest on that lawyer Davey?"

Those around the table were at attention immediately. "He worked for your husband, did he not?"

"To our shame. He used the respectability of our name to win that case. But finally, he has been exposed! They have published an inventory of other offenses too long to name. Of course, he can't even practice anymore – not until he is investigated, and he will definitely have his license revoked when he is found."

"I heard that they will never find him because he jumped a ship: stowed-away and went to Europe."

"Of course, he could. When one has misappropriated such a huge amount, travel expenses are already covered."

"He could easily start afresh with that small fortune in his pocket. One can generally find all sorts of willing participants for a new life under those circumstances."

"Huh. Well, I heard he went native and he's just living with the Blacks in the scrub somewhere."

"That would make sense. What sort of future could anyone in these circumstances have now? How far he has fallen! Last season he was voted 'most eligible bachelor'. That was quite the profile... but now? Completely disgraced! No one will ever touch him again."

"There is a handsome fee to be collected for any who can offer information on those he is riding with... and where he is hiding."

"Handsome fee? What about his handsome face!"

"Do you remember last year's ball? He does have a fetching look about him in a suit. It is a shame. And what a waste! I would have him in my parlour for tea, disgraced or not!" They giggled and tittered, and Abby stood up and brought over some fresh cake.

"Would you like to see the new fabrics I had Sorensen bring in from Winnicott's new range? There are some fine linens, cottons, and a very special bolt of silk – the most exquisite shade of bluebell. I will get Glady to bring them out. Perhaps you can advise me on what garments to make up?"

She summoned her seamstress, and the parade of fabrics began. Each lady oohed and ahhed. They gave their glowing approval and offered a considered opinion on what fashionable ensembles should be made from such extravagance. Pinch-pleats seemed to be the consensus.

⁓⁓⁓❦⁓⁓⁓

5.

After a week of being inundated with visitors, Abby felt completely exhausted. It was a relief to see the convoy roll out, and to close up the guest rooms until next time. Sorensen also left with the assertion he would not be away long this time, barely a couple of weeks: he just had to follow up on some business that had been initiated on saddleback around his paddocks.

Abby sat on the verandah overlooking the garden and then stood up promptly and went to find Callie and the housekeeper. "I fear we have a few things that are entirely not to my liking anymore. I think it would be appropriate to have an update. Mrs Hamill, I want you to consider what you think can be replaced in the linen press and household items, and Callie can help me with my wardrobe. I can have Glady make up more fashionable dresses with the new fabric I have, so there are items here that need to be culled."

Callie and Mrs Hamill looked at Abby quite puzzled.

"Is something wrong? You must admit... having those ladies here made me realise that fashion is an ever-changing phenomenon," Abby shrugged carelessly.

Callie tilted her head. "Ma'am, you have never bothered about those things before. Why is it now so very urgent?"

"*Now* is always the appropriate time to see improvements made. So, let us get started."

She went into her wardrobe and looked around. Callie pulled out a flimsy old-fashioned impractical dress that was a very dull green. Abby glanced at it and quickly put it back. "I don't mind that; let's look at the cotton dresses."

Callie raised her brow. Had her mistress lost her mind? "You never wear that dress Ma'am."

"True. Okay. I will get rid of it too."

Every dress made of cotton quickly became obsolete.

"Ma'am... I don't understand. Why are you getting rid of all of these?"

"I need to update. Cotton is such a practical hard-wearing type of material."

"You have always preferred it for that very reason. Ma'am, I cannot believe this. It seems such a waste."

Abby smiled. "Having these dresses sitting here gathering dust is the real waste. I will discard them, and then... wherever we put them... wherever they go... and whoever finds them, they will be out of my way, and it will not be my concern."

"Ohh..." said Callie, thinking that perhaps her mistress had not gone completely barmy after all.

"And perhaps," Abby added for clarification, "...even if someone cut off the outer skirts to make up clothes for their children or some of them are used to replace worn out dresses... it is no matter to me. I will not miss them."

"Ohh... well in that case, it does seem agreeable Ma'am, how it could be needful for you to stay updated."

"And it is imperative for Sorensen to have a new wardrobe as well. He is an important man of society, so to be presentable is an essential aspect of his responsibilities."

"Yes Ma'am. He is indeed an important person."

"For his old clothes, I would consider it appropriate to dump them right out of the way, so that our station workers don't pick them up. I wouldn't think Sorensen would like to see the stockmen wearing his town shirts. Perhaps the boundary waste-tip would be far enough away."

Callie bobbed a curtsy and smothered a smile. "Yes Ma'am, that is a long way away".

"I will send a message to Winnicott's with a list of new items for his tailor to make up. They have his measurements on file. He definitely needs some new suits while he is in town. This is an entirely good idea."

6.

Callie brought the breakfast tray into the room and put it on the side table. She went to the window and opened the drapes. Abby rolled over and rubbed her eyes. "Oh Callie, I didn't expect you today. I told you to take an extra day. Sorenson's trip is taking longer than expected. I had a message from Gillis that he does not return until next week."

"You did say that Ma'am. Yes."

Abby sat up. "So, what happened? Is everything all right? How is Ted?"

"Doing well Ma'am. Very well. The salt baths are working." She pulled out a folded piece of paper from her pinafore pocket and lowered her voice. "This is for you, Ma'am."

"Me? That's curious." She took note and opened it up. She blinked, folded it, and handed it back to her. "Hmm. You are right – that is *very* curious."

"Do you think so, Ma'am?"

"Yes. When you go back up there this morning, please pass on my apologies."

"But Ma'am, I thought the note was a courteous gesture."

"Then I will write a note to that effect if you prefer. You can take the things he requests with you."

"Yes Ma'am. If, you are sure."

"I am." And she folded back the covers and went straight to her desk and wrote out her apology. She handed it to Callie. "Please go now and make sure this is delivered with the greatest promptness. And give my regards to Ted. Leave the tray, I will attend to it."

Abby got on with her day and dealt with every household matter with her usual efficiency. She spoke serenely to Glady about making up some additional tablecloths and serviettes for the upcoming Shearers Ball. She talked with Gillis about the status of a couple of the workers whose children were sick with fevers and rashes. She asked Cook to make up some broth and reallocated one of the maids to deliver it to them. She also made sure that the mothers had additional help while the children were being nursed.

Yet, even with all this routine industry, inside Abby felt completely off balance. The bold handwriting on the note from Callie's pocket loomed large. She tried to push it away, but it refused to stay hidden in her mind. She wished he had been rude, or demanding, or painfully intent on misusing her compassion, or aggressively bemoaning his impoverished circumstances. If he had been any of those things, it would not be difficult to be dismissive in reply. However, the tone of respect in his appeal made it impossible to ignore. It had completely... ambushed her! Was *ambush* his memorandum operands? Was she just following the precedent set by the Inland Case? It felt like it.

She picked up her scissors and a shallow basket and took a deep breath as she stepped out onto the sweeping verandah downstairs. What was she to do? She could only do what she was already doing. Painfully, that was her only option. Regardless of whether she wanted to run to the hills and find refuge in that cavern of respect, Redwood Park was her life. She had to resolutely follow the course that had been set before her. Well, the precedent had been made. She would be respectful in all her dealings; even her refusal to get involved. She was grateful Mr Davey had been so explicit in his prohibition of her going near his camp. That, at least, gave her a logical course of action. She was just following his directive.

The mid-morning sun was already warm, and Abby adjusted her hat and took a glass of cool water from the tray sitting on the verandah table. She sipped it and noticed how respect offered so much relief. It was just a note, yet it was like this glass of cool water, refreshing and life-giving. She set the glass back on the tray and determinedly walked down the steps out into the garden. If she could not be a recipient of respect in her marriage, she could be a carrier of respect in her household. A water-carrier of refreshment.

Right now, her mission was to pick some flowers for the drawing room. A vase of blooms always made the aspect of a room brighter and cleaner. She paused and picked a gardenia... fragile, beautiful, and fragrant. The waxy white petals easily bruise, and she felt the bruises under her dress, as she looked at the perfect spiral at the centre of the flower, smelling divine! She swallowed, and decided a simple arrangement is what she needed today. She added some greenery to her basket and turned along a side garden looking for dog-roses to add to her collection.

Suddenly a grubby hand clamped over her mouth, and she was pulled back into the shadows of a hedgerow. The basket scattered its contents over the lawn as she fought and wriggled but there was no escaping such a brute of a frame. Then she caught sight of her captor's boots; boots that were from the discarded Sorensen pile. Oh. She went limp and stopped resisting, waiting until she was released. She stood up and smoothed her skirts and hair, turned around and looked expectantly at her captor.

Dickens' rough face bore a grin. "Morning Ma'am. Mister Ruben requests your attendance." He straightened up and tucked his thumbs into his belt to show her that he wore Sorensen's braces and one of his old vests. He looked very pleased with the acquisitions.

"But I have already sent an apology. I gave the note to Callie and asked her to deliver it this morning when she went visiting."

"Well, he said to me, Ma'am: it is less like an invitation, and more like a direct request. He expects you to attend."

"Then it is not a request. That is a command."

"If you think so, Ma'am."

Abby sighed. After all her deliberations, this is not what she needed. "So, what is going on?"

"What do you mean Ma'am?"

"Why does he need to see me so categorically? I sent the things he asked for with Callie."

"He will explain it, Ma'am. I just do as he asks."

She adjusted her hat. "Well, this is awkward to say the least. He told me to stay away. Very well. I will get some water and have my horse saddled."

"No need Ma'am. You are to come with me."

"Now?

"Yes Ma'am."

They rode out on a different route, well away from the dump. Dickens paused at a certain point and turned around and nodded to her.

"Blindfold?"

"Yes Ma'am. From here, if you don't mind."

"And even if I do mind, I am to comply," she murmured, as she closed her eyes and tied up her scarf firmly. Her curiosity wanted to be satisfied, and she considered leaving her scarf a little loose so she could see. But she reminded herself of Ruben's sensible strategy. Not having to pretend ignorance, was to her advantage.

She adjusted to the sway of the saddle and clung on to Dickens as the horse stepped upwards over the rough terrain. When they stopped, she felt hands lift her down. She was led over and taken inside a shelter. Those hands loosened the tie over her eyes, and she looked up into the face of Ruben Davey. She was back at his 'quarters'.

She took the scarf from his hands and stepped back, taking in more details of where he lived. Sparse. The lamp on the table was cracked. The table was made from a cartwheel rim. There was a journal that had the look of a ship captain's log, and a very chipped writing set. A shelf held a few worn books, as well as a Bible. His bunk was made tidily, although it looked hard and uncomfortable. No feather comforters here. Overall, it had the feel of a robber's den in the manner and style of Ali Baba, without the treasure.

"My apologies for the drama, Mrs Bates. But it was apparently necessary since you declined my invitation."

"You are the one who told me so very adamantly to stay away."

His eyes did not change as they looked into her face. "So, one would then assume, that if I sent for you, something sufficiently significant had happened for me to change my mind, absorb the risk and warrant your presence."

"Oh, this has got to be good."

"I wish it were. Nothing would give me more pleasure than to offer you High Tea on my verandah overlooking our spectacular outlook. But this is not a social call."

She inhaled quickly. He alluded to her routine. How much surveillance did he have on her life?

"Oh come, that can't really be a surprise to you. I know enough to suspect you are neither malicious in your nature nor devious in your intent. The company you keep may be less so."

"I have come to the conclusion, Mr Davey, that I am not responsible for the intentions of those I keep company with... only my own."

"Which brings us to our current predicament. I have a man who was shot. I need you to tend him. Like you did with Ted."

"Shot! How?"

"Does it matter? The end result is the same. He was only winged, so I had no fear for his life. He was doing all right, but I am now concerned that infectious corruption is setting in. He needs proper care."

"And *I* am the one to do this? He should go to a doctor."

"A doctor? And how would we pay for professional services? Never mind getting him there without exposing our position."

"You brought me here. I wouldn't think this is beyond your resourcefulness, Mr Davey."

"You spent a great deal of time ranting about your abilities last time you were here: nursing your father-in-law. You insisted you were more than just a pretty face capable of pouring a nice cup of tea. I offer you the opportunity to support this idea, Mrs Bates. If you would be so kind."

"My father-in-law was aged and infirm. His skin would bruise when he fell. But it is very different dressing grazes and cuts, to a violent bullet wound that you say is turning septic."

"Please have a look – the principles are probably transferable."

"Mr Davey, I feel the responsibility keenly," she said with a shake of her head.

"Good," he said, unmoved.

"I was going to add that there might be nothing I can offer that will make any difference."

"I don't expect you to impart a miraculous healing. Our responsibility is to do everything we can, pray for a good outcome and leave the result in the domain of the Divine."

"Very well." She was not pleased to be placed in such an untenable position. She regretted her pride had oversold her capabilities as a nurse.

Ruben took her to the hut where Ted had been. She looked at the man on the mat. He was dozing and she choked at the smell. Flies were buzzing around the dressing on his shoulder. "What is his name, Mr Davey?"

"Joseph Hills."

"Does he go by Joseph or Joe?"

"Jay."

She held her breath and leant over him. "Jay? Can you open your eyes for me? I have come to have a look at your arm. Jay? Open your eyes."

Ruben prodded him with the toe of his boot. "Oi! Jay! Look sharp. I have someone here to look at your wound."

Abby stared at Ruben's worn boots. He obviously distributed the cast-off clothing through the camp to his men, but had not taken any items for himself? She frowned at the thought and then drew her attention back to the man in front of her. "Jay? I'm going to take down your dressing now."

She turned to Ruben. "I will need a bowl of warm water and another bucket of fresh water. If you have salt left, bring me that." She closed her eyes, bracing herself, as he directed someone to fetch it. She started peeling away the putrid layers. She gagged as she saw maggots wriggling around the bandages. "Have you not been changing this at all? I told you what was needed with Ted. Why hasn't this been attended to? This neglect means you may as well have shot him yourself!" Jay pulled away as she tore up some rag and started swabbing down the red and inflamed entry wound with water. "I'm going to need two of your men to hold him. Make sure one is Dickens, and the other of comparative size and strength. He is not going to like this." She started again, and then quickly stood up and went outside and was sick.

Ruben followed her outside. "Can you do this? Did I overestimate you?"

She straightened up and looked him in the eye. "I may have overstated my experience, but not my compassion. If a weak constitution is a crime, then I am guilty. I will do what I can to clean it up. There is no exit wound, so I believe the bullet is still in there. I do think you need to consider finding a medical man... or a nurse."

"That is not an option."

"Do you value your man's life at all?"

"Very much. I also value every other man here. There are fifteen I am responsible for. Not all are here at once of course. A few come and go. Still, in some places that is a village. I cannot risk their lives because some landed gentleman thinks he is hunting game and shoots at my man."

She stared at him hard. "Gentleman? Sorensen?"

"I don't think it was intentional. A misfortune perhaps."

"That is a generous assessment, Mr Davey. I appreciate it."

"You don't think this was accidental?"

"I know my husband. If he had a clear enough sight of anyone whom he thought was encroaching his territory... black or white, he would shoot – not just to maim. Jay is fortunate."

"You accuse me of being hard, but you are a hard woman if you can make such a cold charge against the one you chose to share your life with. If Jay dies..."

"Cold... or realistic? Not everyone has the choices available to them that you have, Mr Davey. I will do all I can to see that Jay is given every opportunity to recover."

He considered her for a bit. He had not thought his position in the hills was like choosing from a smorgasbord of options. "The colour has come back to your face. I will assist you in your endeavour to remove the pellet. It seems Jay is condemned one way or another. We will do what we can and pray to God Almighty for his grace and mercy."

"You are chieftain of this village, Mr Davey. I will do my best again... to right a wrong."

"My intention, Mrs Bates, was to get Jay some help. Not make you pay for your husband's crimes. If you are willing to help, I would appreciate it. Otherwise, you are released to go."

"Released?"

He nodded. "You may go... if this is too much to expect. I will not presume to impose on your aid again."

"Well, thank you. I am generally not given a choice. Were I to choose between my inclination for clean air or being of some useful service, then I prefer the idea of service. I would like to help. But you are now aware: you do not get too much skill for your trouble to bring me here."

That made him smile, slightly, with a hint of irony. "How about we don't disclose your inexperience and allow their ignorance offer my men some hope."

"You would have me perjure myself?"

"No more than you have already. Let us get to this. Sound confident. Be bossy. I know you can do that. It will work to their favour, for these men are afraid for their mate."

❧❧❧

7

Abby had been surrounded by unsympathetic dictators all her life. Her resolution was to be different: to be the peacemaker rather than an antagonist; to influence with kindness rather than oppress with force. And now she had added another quality: to offer respect, even when her life was bombarded with contempt and insolence. Ruben's instruction to be bossy for mere dramatic effect, felt like regression. Yet experience had taught her, that proficiency in presenting something on the face of it, other than what was real, was sometimes necessary. This was more than just acting. It was survival. Abby took a deep breath and removed her scarf and wrapped it around her waist as an apron. Then she plunged back into the hut. "Come gentlemen, time is of the essence! Jay, this is going to be hard. Are you up for this?"

He nodded through his fever.

"You need to hold his arm and his body. Sit on his legs. If he thrashes it will injure him further." She bathed the area. She brushed away the flies and found the wound was cleaner than she expected as she irrigated the maggots away. She supressed the reflex to gag and tried to think what this would mean if it was a fly-blown sheep. She knew of the problem, but she had no idea how the shepherds managed it. It seemed her prayer for 'transferable' information had no basis on which to start. She knew nursing basics, but mostly Old Mr Bates just wanted the attentions of a pretty girl who was not a common maid. His military rank had given him a predilection for privilege, and his social arrogances were not serving her at all in this situation. Then she thought of one of her father's hunting dogs who had licked his wounds after being gashed by a pig's tusk. The dog was too valuable to be put down immediately, and although, as a young girl she thought it was disgusting, it was the general observation in the weeks that ensured, that the dog's licking action helped heal his leg well enough to be put back into service. So that is what she went with. Just like Ted's open cuts, they had to make this wound clean, and keep it clean. As she swabbed, she could feel an uneven lump... fragment of bone perhaps... or bullet... lying in the muscle. Not deep. The shot had not been at close range, so it was either a remarkably well-aimed hit, or incredibly bad luck that a stray bullet had struck him at random.

"Mr Davey, I'm sure I can feel the pellet. Just here. I need you to try and put tension on the muscle as I extract it. Hold it there. Pass me those forceps. Gentlemen: Hold him firmly. Jay bite down on the razor strap. This is going to be nasty. Bite down. Focus on the leather! Hold his legs still, Mr Hawk. I can feel it again! Yes! Here it is. That is quite the trophy, Mr Hills. Well done, Gentlemen!"

She irrigated the wound firmly, and trimmed the fraying flesh around the ragged edges, swabbing the bleeding. "Dickens, watch what I am doing here. You need to do this three times a day. Burn the old bandages, wash it down with salted water as you did for Ted. I will send up some tinctures that I have at home. Follow the instructions and put about five drops inside the wound each time. Wrap it firmly. I am afraid it will not heal prettily, but it will leave an interesting scar with a story to tell." She didn't want to think about what would happen if the rot was too deeply embedded to actually heal. Some old-timers thought that maggots were a positive thing and helped keep flesh clean. Well, if they had done their part, and she had done hers, perhaps as Ruben suggested... the result was in the hand of the Divine.

Abby washed her hands firmly and went outside. She leant over and threw-up in the bushes again. When she was done, she stood leaning hard against a tree looking out over the valley below them. She saw the tiny outline of the Redwood Park's homestead and outbuildings and wondered how two worlds could be so far apart. It seemed inexplicable to her that she was traversing both realms, and comfortable in neither.

She heard a step behind her and straightened up. She turned and nodded with a half-smile. "Was that bossy enough for you, Mr Davey?"

He handed her a drink of water in a chipped enamel mug. "Exceptionally so. Jay thanks you. I know that wasn't easy. I will take you back now."

"You? *You* can't take me back."

"I can. I was hoping to look at your library. There is a particular reference that I am interesting in. I was wanting to borrow it. And paper and ink if you have any to spare. I am just about out. I am working on my defence."

"You want to be reinstated after what they did to you?"

"More interested in clearing my name. Crimes are being added against my reputation which I have had nothing to do with."

"Do not all criminals claim innocence?"

"I am determined to fight fair even when others pull no punches. Despite all, I am a great believer in the justice of law and good prevailing."

"Doesn't that seem a little naïve, given the circumstances you find yourself in? Isn't this evidence against the reality of ever winning such a war? The tide of opinion is certainly against you."

He smiled. "My education suggests that facts rather than public opinion, should dictate the charges, and determine the sentence. I believe it was you who observed that I have choices at my disposal. And you are right. This is my current choice. It serves me for now. These hills are not proof of failure but allows me time to identify a pathway through the impossible."

"How can you still have faith to believe in the impossible when you live like this?"

"People said the very same thing about the court-case you so elegantly referred to. They said such an outcome was impossible. But impossible just means it hasn't been accomplished yet. Yet now that it has been done, it is no longer remarkable. Now the law demands that white men will have to answer to the court for crimes against people regardless of colour. Now there is a precedence set that they have the right of being acknowledged before a court of law."

"It was a bold stone to throw, Mr Davey."

"Not really. My anger just got bigger than my complacency or fear. Respectable people declared it was improper. But it was the right stone to throw, and I was fortunate enough that it hit its target. Justice is not perfected in this arena by any means. But it is a start. Now we are headed in the right direction."

"You are a humble man if you can win such a battle and take so little credit."

"I think I was positioned at the right time. Injustice is a strong motivator for me. Right now, I am at that angry place again. And although I believe the Lord is my vindicator, I need to work on my own great battle. This fight in some respects is harder because the lines are less clear. That... and the fact it is personal. I remind myself that I am also permitted justice, just like every other client I have fought for. But

I am aware that aspects of the truth are hidden so deep in my case that I find it difficult not to despair of it ever coming to light."

"Our library is not a professional resource. How do you know the book you want will be there?"

"I don't. I am working on the assumption that it is usual for any gentleman's library to hold books that look good on the shelf but are never read. It is a long shot, but Jay is witness to the fact that even long shots can hit their target. There are gaps that I need to address, and this may be a path to that end. When you are ready, Mrs Bates, I will take you back to your husband's home."

"It is my home too."

"Hmm. You don't seem so comfortable there. More like a visitor, or an intern, detained on a good behaviour bond."

"It befalls me to do the best that I can, with the life that I have."

"Ahh! And *that* I think is the first point of agreement that I have found with you, Mrs Bates. With all our differences, our fates are the same."

He hoisted her up onto the horse and they left. Abby felt so flustered, that as he turned out along a barely visible kangaroo-track, she didn't even realise he had forgotten to apply the blindfold.

⁓⊹⊱✦⊰⊹⁓

8.

"Oh Sorenson! You are here! How was your trip? Fruitful, I presume since you are back much sooner than anticipated."

"Bah! The opposite. Where have you been?" He came over and turned up his nose. "Grief woman you stink! Don't come in here reeking like horse stables!" He swore in disgust.

"I have been out in the garden. And I did spend some time with horses today."

"Whatever for? A proper woman leaves that to the lackeys."

"I enjoy a ride to get out now and then. We could go riding together sometime perhaps."

"Bah! I have important matters to attend to. I'm not here for long. I leave again in the morning. I have to cover some things with Gillis and then I'm gone."

"Your overseer gets more of your time than I do. When will you return?" She hoped it sounded like the longing wife. It suited his sense of importance to be missed.

"Gillis earns his keep, so of course he gets my time. I'll be back when business is done and not before. Gee this room is dark and dingy! Talk to Hamill about attending to her duties properly. Do I have to do your job as well as mine?" He impatiently went to the French doors and pulled back the heavy drapes.

Abby almost audibly gasped. She had told Mr Davey she would unlock the latch and then pull back the curtains as a sign he could access the library. She quickly went over and closed the drapes again. That was a bold move. "I heard that sunlight pouring into a library damages the books. You have valuable volumes here worth protecting."

"Idiotic notion! I need a decent amount of light. Close them when I am gone!" He swore emphatically as he opened them again. "Now be gone with you. I have work to do!" He was irritated and Abby knew it was risky to overlook the signs.

"I will open the doors to see if that will clear the dingy atmosphere and circulate fresh air for you." She went and latched back the French doors and shook the fabric of the curtains. "Perhaps you are right. I will speak to Mrs Hamill about washing these drapes." She quickly stepped out onto the verandah and rubbed her forehead and spoke out over the garden. "Sorensen, I will call for Cook to bring you refreshments here in the library so you can continue to work undisturbed."

"What has got into you? Stop fussing and let me do my work!"

"It is different when you are gone. That is all."

"Shearing starts soon. I'll be around then."

Abby walked slowly back to the kitchen. She didn't know how else to warn Mr Davey that the curtain-sign had been inadvertently intercepted by Sorensen's unexpected return. She never took too much notice of the library before. It was Sorensen's domain and that didn't interest her... perhaps even disgusted her. She had her own collection of books in her private parlour. But now that Mr Davey desired access to the library, suddenly it was more interesting.

She spoke to Cook and directed her to deliver Sorensen's refreshments through the French doors facing the verandah. Perhaps that would be another sign. It would have to be enough.

Sorensen attended to his business in the library and then adjourned to his office; ate his meal in silence; went to bed late; rose early to leave. Abby did everything to make life smooth. And it was.

When the universe revolved around Sorensen's orbit, all was as it should be.

⁂

Abby walked along the verandah and looked out over the garden, drenched in soft drizzle. This life was as grey as the clouds, but the freshness in the smell of rain comforted her. It felt washed. It was watering the plants in her garden, allowing life to grow. It started to rain again; she went back into the library. She pulled back the curtains and propped open the doors allowing the smell of fresh rain to run through the room. Mr Davey, at least, had not been accosted, even if his plan to access study references had been aborted. Sorenson would not be above collecting the bounty on his head. Ah, the tag bushranger was unfair, and completely inaccurate. She sat down in the reading chair opposite his desk and looked at the shelves that held so many books. Most of these books had been collected by Sorensen's father, and had stood on these shelves for decades unread, their ideas locked between their covers. She wondered if she were to choose a book, which volume would attract her attention. She stood up and wandered around the bookshelves. She had never noticed the range of subjects held on these shelves before. She picked a book that had a benign sort of title: 'Literary Sketches of a Pastoral Maid' and she opened it up. The front insert had an inscription – it had been a gift to Sorensen's mother. She read a page or two, but found the language stilted, and the ideas clumsy. That was not attractive to her at all. Perhaps you *could* tell a book by its title. Or at least get a very good hint of it. She put it back.

"That was not to your liking then?"

She jolted. Mr Davey stood by the door in his oiled all-weather coat and hat. He stepped inside and water dripped off the brim of his hat onto the polished timber floor. He barely acknowledged the puddles but took off his jacket and hat as she nodded a greeting. "I am grateful you understood the change of circumstances. Discussing books may not have been the main point of an encounter with Sorensen in his library."

"Discussion is not my aim either. I won't trespass your hospitality long," he said stiffly as he moved away from the door.

"I will leave it to you then. I will air the room, and then come back later to close it up."

"Yes. Would not do to have a library smelling of horses."

She looked at him curiously, nodded with a slight smile, and turned to leave.

"Oh. Mrs Bates... before you go?"

"Yes?"

"Could I make one more imposition? I would have you write a note, confirming you have authorised borrowing these volumes and that they will be returned. Should they be found in my possession, a misunderstanding could tip the scales towards a rope, even though we have an agreement that this is merely a short-term loan. If you would keep a copy yourself, it would be appreciated."

"Oh! Yes. Of course. Don't want you to become acquainted with a noose, for the sake of a book that had sat idle for so long." She sat down and wrote; then folded the paper. "Mr Davey, shearing is to start soon, and the station will be swarming with people. Many of these people are strangers to us and I cannot vouch for their trustworthiness."

"Do you caution me for my benefit, or are you merely concerned for your own reputation?"

"My reputation and your safety appear to be both matters that would benefit from your discretion."

"I am always careful, Mrs Bates. There are eyes and ears on every tree. Although I believe we are establishing a level of credibility with the locals."

She stood and nodded. Not that she really understood what he meant by that. She paused as the rain became a little heavier, and she closed the French doors and pulled the curtains before she handed the over paper. "You are right, Mr Davey, in limiting the exposure to eyes and ears... even if they belong to the woodlands. The stationery and ink you requested have been entrusted to Callie."

He nodded.

Abby paused at the door. "I was going to have some tea. Would you like me to bring you a cup? Just while you find the volumes you were looking for."

He nodded gravely as he started looking at the shelves of books.

Abby went and made up a tray. She had Cook cut some bread. When she came back, he was sitting at the desk, the lamp lit, looking though a couple of substantial volumes, very much at home in the realm of books and study.

He stood up and came over and sat at her invitation. "This is very generous, Mrs Bates."

"You look after your men. It is something I admire," she said as she poured him a cup.

"I believe that loyalty is engendered by fairness and consideration rather than an inadequate pay-cheque under the threat of dismissal or a lashing."

"I think you try to conceive a world that is entirely not possible, Mr Davey."

"Does not the Scripture say that all things are possible to them that believe?"

"I do not consider myself to be entirely without faith, but what you speak of... it seems so far from the actual experience of life, that I have to wonder who could dream of things so magnificent."

"It is necessary to dream of a world like that. It is what keeps me going... it keeps me breathing."

"And yet you are living as a fugitive in the caverns of the Gilyard Range. That is hard and rough and remote!"

"Still, my men are loyal... to a fault. And as unlikely as it seems, the fact that it is hard and rough and remote becomes our protection."

"I will persist in suggesting you are not living your dream, Mr Davey."

"My dream? Perhaps, but I am living the pathway towards it. Mrs Bates, I am the first to acknowledge it is not fair, nor comfortable. Most men of God in the Bible had their periods of exile or wilderness: Jacob, Joseph, Moses, Joshua, David, Daniel. Even Jesus, Paul, and John. I stand in the company of a long list of remarkable men."

"Remarkable indeed. Possibly you are one of them, after all."

"My understanding is that it was not remarkable that they were exiled, or even that some of them were promoted afterwards. Only that, in the waiting, they excelled where they were, for that time. They believed the vision of a better future during the in-between time. 'Things yet unseen'. That was their noteworthy achievement: The Meantime."

Abby cast her eyes low. Maybe he was right. She had her own wilderness, her own *Meantime.* "So, you believe it is entirely reasonable to hope for a time where justice is no longer based on occupation, or skin colour, or culture, or even gender... but slavery is considered a general abomination, even if it is dressed in a shearers' singlet and moccasins, or a corset and a skirt? Would you conceive a world where women could choose an occupation and their spouse, rather than being traded like breeding ewes? Where the little people have a voice that is heard and can hold an opinion that is esteemed? It seems like an extravagant aspiration, Mr Davey."

"It is the extravagance of the ambition that makes it *Faith*, Mrs Bates. But perhaps inroads in the smallest of ways support the grandeur of the destination. After all, you have opinions that you give voice to. In fact, my observation is that you don't seem to have any problem speaking your thoughts at all."

She shrugged. "Perhaps that is entirely dependent on the audience. I have been known to falter."

"But still, isn't this small step the beginning of an entire journey in the right direction?"

"Perhaps you speak of the same hope I have endeavoured to live by. Every incremental shift towards right, is a response to wrong." She pointed to the untouched tray of sandwiches. "Please, Mr Davey – do eat. I have seen your menu and your cook. I cannot believe that you are not tempted."

"I was wanting to take some back with me," he said matter-of-factly.

"For your men? Now what would they want with freshly baked bread, roasted lamb and Cook's legendary pickled onions?"

He grinned. "If I tell them, I could well be faced with mutiny."

"So, another factor in generating loyalty is fresh bread, and excellent condiments! Don't be shy. I have asked Cook to make up some extra for you as you take your leave. They will not be left wanting. This portion is for you."

That was the only encouragement that was needed. Soon all that was left on the plate was crumbs, and his second cup of tea was gone. He stood up. "I think for now, these three books will get me started."

There was a knock at the door and Cook handed over a flour bag filled with the promised loot. He went to his coat, and produced another bag, carefully wrapping up the books in canvas before he tucked them away. When Abby turned around again, his coat and hat had disappeared with him, and all that was left was a water stain on the floorboards. Abby went and locked the library door.

❦

9.

Shearing time is the sheep-graziers' harvest. It is a time that is noisy from early morning to late evening, full of hectic schedules, tallies and counts, and industrious optimism. Crews appeared and made their presence felt. Redwood Park became a small city. The homestead guestrooms were filled once more as wool classers, accountants and bankers came to be part the spectacle. Musterers, shed-hands, pressers, bullockies, mess crews, and anyone who could hold a pair of shears was put into service. The demand for good shearers would always be a practical issue on the larger spreads. Even Ted made an appearance on the board because he was able to hold his own with a reasonable tally. Gillis admitted him only after he had extracted a sworn oath that he would keep his red head down and his temper in check.

There was a lot of talk about the menial conditions that the shearers were subject to, and the introduction of mechanical shears. This invention was the controversy that had been the centre of Ted's public shaming. But the arguments of the impacts of automation against the talk of trials already being conducted at some stations fell on deaf ears. Sorensen doggedly continued to publish his enthusiastic support of automation and was determined to install mechanical shears as soon as they were available. He was a pastoralist who was determined to keep the reputation of his operation commercially 'progressive'.

Life always sped up for the duration of shearing season. Abby had perfected the skill of staying sufficiently visible to allay any attention. It was a relief that no one had use for a mantelpiece ornament during shearing season, and she had time to attend to her own responsibilities undisturbed while the focal point of the universe shifted to the shed.

When the last wether was sent stumbling down the shoot, shorn and skinny, a cheer rose from the board and the men carefully totalled their tallies for the final count, as every mark was gold to them. The shearer who achieved the shed record revelled in his short stint as a celebrity, being the immediate recipient of a generous round of drinks. Bullock drays were loaded with the large square bales of wool stacked high. The bullockies chipped out their commands with a crack of the whip, as they moved their teams out along the road, straining under the weight of the spoils of war. It was the victory parade after a great battle.

A Shearer's Ball was held to mark the end of every season. This had been a particularly prosperous year, so it was therefore incumbent of Sorensen Bates to have the largest, most lavish event of any shearing shed in the valley. Where other spreads around may pull an all-night bash to mark the close of the shearing, the Redwood Park Ball, as it was known, went on for days. The term 'Ball' – reminiscent of the English gentry, was entirely too generous, but all-in-all it was a substantial binge on food, with a healthy smattering of competitive happenings. The events were arranged to include the community of the station: children's races, whip-cracking, cake-baking, jam-making. The music was loud; the dancing exuberant; and it was helped along with a fair allocation of lubricating ale. The carnival atmosphere started out strong, but as appetites faded and the drinks dulled minds and feelings, there were fewer treats offered to the masses. The food reverted to plain damper, spit-roasted lamb, and simply more ale. And no one minded too much. If the men had their tankards refilled, and the kids had enough sugar to throw-up on their feet, then everyone was happy. The women took the opportunity to catch up on social chin-wagging and retreated out of the way, for a few days of respite.

The main event for Bates was hosting the lavish Shearer's Feast on the third day of the festival. It was an exclusive spread for the overseers, local dignitaries, and society notables... and their wives. The inside of the shearing shed was transformed into a large banquet hall bedecked with lanterns and garlands around the rafters, still smelling of fleece and lanolin. Trestle tables were set with cloths and candles, illuminating the shed in a beautiful glow while the rabble continued to party uninhibited outside into the night.

Abby sat with Sorensen at the head table, dressed elegantly in her new bluebell silk gown, pin-pleats across the bodice. Sorensen bemoaned the cost of the occasion under his breath, and loudly lapped up the silver-tongued accolades from his guests with all the humility of a peacock. He proceeded to entertain his guests with all sorts of stories of unparalleled challenge and triumph. No matter what the account, Sorensen featured as the shining hero in gold-plated armour.

Ruben waited until this renowned third day of the festivities, when the Feast was in full swing, as he supposed that Bates' spirits would be elevated and the social pressure to be generous would be high. Then he sent a delegation of three men to deliver Bates a letter. Sorensen sat at the table and looked at the men as if they were circus oddities. "Sir, we are here to deliver a letter. It is our hope to have a response before we return."

Abby adverted her eyes. She did not want to make eye contact with Dickens or his mates. Dickens was still wearing Sorenson's vest, and his boots. But she didn't fear too much on that score. They were now worn, scuffed and grubby. She doubted that Sorenson would recognise them as items from his wardrobe.

Sorensen stood; and came around to them. "Well ladies and gentlemen, the entertainment has come to us. Let's see what they have for us." He spoke expansively to his guests with a jovial lilt. He noticed the guests had stopped eating so he took the letter from Dickens' hand with a flourish. Abby cringed again. It was written on the paper she had given Ruben, but it was generic enough to be unrecognisable. Sorensen had his own embossed stationery that was his preference. He flicked it open and smiled at his guests. "Let's see... *'Dear Sir, Congratulations on your successful shear...'* Blah, blah, blah... an appropriate sort of salutation I suppose. Let's skip all that. Here... this is interesting. *'As you know your property and stock have not suffered loss from the duffing wave that has dogged other properties around the district. You can confirm with your men our contribution to your position. We wish to reassure you of our ongoing surveillance of your resources and consider it our privilege to align with your operation in this synergistic partnership. As festivities wrap up the Shearing, we would respectfully ask for anything you could offer our men as a token of this happy time.'"* Sorensen's face had gone dark. His eyes flashed, and the pitch of his voice lowered. Abby ducked her head and swallowed. She knew these signs. He turned to them and growled. Instinctively they stepped back. "Privilege? Who signs this rubbish?" He scanned the letter again. "... *'Yours sincerely, Capt. Red, endorsing Rights, Entitlements and Decency as our common human experience.'* That tells me nothing! This Captain Red flaunts his knowledge of my position, and yet conceals his own identity like some criminal hiding in the hills to escape an irreparable reputation!"

Abby swallowed again. So, he knew? All this time he knew they were there. She stood up and came over to Sorensen, full of charm and loveliness. "Sorensen dear, let me take care of this. These men are really not worthy of your bother when you are hosting important guests, begging your hospitality. You should finish telling how you managed to secure your stallion. I was hoping they would hear that whole story. Don't allow this to interrupt you."

He looked at her and his eyes narrowed. There was a reptilian coldness in his gaze that she was familiar with, but she didn't cringe. She merely smiled at their guests. "Did you not want to hear the outcome? Are you not curious to know what incredible stroke of genius secured his famed Arabian?"

The guests vaguely applauded the suggestion but then immediately turned back to their conversations peppered with questions about this interruption. Their interest focused on whether this Red was indeed Ruben Davey, the famed social-advocate-gone-bad? Of course, it had to be. Did Bates have access to him all along? Was he actually in cahoots with the infamous lawyer turned bushranger? Perhaps Bates had hired him, as the letter suggested, contracting as some sort of security service. There was no doubt the losses other places had suffered was not part of the Redwood shearing experience. Why else would there be such an ostentatious display of his success? Perhaps Bates was behind those crooks... and the raids on other properties directly benefitted him, plumping out his own herds.

Bates could hear the speculation around the table starting to escalate. There were a couple of points that irked him: The attention was diverted; the momentum of his story had been derailed; there was innuendo that sullied his gilded reputation. The implication of the unsettled mood around the shed, was that workers should not be bought off by a generously laden dray from the distillery which imported kegs of grog for the event. When it came down to it, Bates was an ugly-drunk. He had consumed enough ale over the last few days, not to make him as amiable as Ruben supposed, but to intensify his sense of conspiracy and paranoia.

He called for his security; he called for Gillis; he called for anyone and everyone to attend to this immediately. He pushed Abby roughly aside and she stumbled back against some barrels and wool bales. Dickens instinctively reached out to help her, but Sorensen immediately hauled him in by the collar and slogged him on the jaw. "Don't you lay a hand on my wife, you despicable piece of carrion!"

Abby scrambled to her feet and went to aid Dickens. Bates roughly pushed her again, swearing profanities at her interference. This time she fell harder. She landed heavily on her hand, twisting it awkwardly as she fell, and she cried out as she heard her wrist crack.

Her husband barely offered her a glance. He was not finished. Abby edged out of the shed and went up to the house so Callie could firmly wrap her hand, pain screaming through her wrist in excruciating waves.

Bates turned on the messengers. "Go tell your Captain Red that I don't partner with felons! I do have a message! And I will give it to you in person." He ordered his men to drag them out into the mustering yards under the light of torches. They tied their hands to the fence rails and then each one was given a flogging with a folded stock whip. "You tell Red *he* is not the one who administers justice. You can assure him, that if any of you vultures show up here again, they will not just get a few cuts across the back! Now crawl back into your holes in the hills and never show up here again!"

Then Bates squared his shoulders, adjusted his jacket, pasted on a smile, and gestured to the spectating guests who gathered around, with an expansive sweep of his hand. "Intermission is over, Ladies and Gentlemen. We have a fine selection of wines and delectable desserts, so please, refill your glasses and let us put this unpleasantness behind us. There is more entertainment to be had." And he called for the musicians to offer an upbeat number and commenced the dancing without delay. Although the interruption was hardly forgotten, it was pushed aside as the program resumed. The evening continued mulled by wine and music.

⚜

10

Gillis held his hat in his hand. "Callie, I need to see Mistress Abby. Don't be causing me grief now."

"You can't. It is too early, and she is lying in this morning." She lowered her voice in distress. "He broke her hand, Gillis! Who does that to his wife? This is not the first time."

"I know. But I need to see her. Now."

"What is it, Gillis?" Abby stood at the door nursing her hand.

"Oh, Ma'am I am sorry to bother you. But I fear this is not going to be good."

"What do you mean? Are the festivities not going well? Are the crews not happy with their supplies?"

"Happy enough. There are some who are trying to stir, but mostly they are well-oiled and forgetting their troubles for now. This is a different sort of trouble."

Her head was pounding, and she rubbed her forehead. She had knocked it hard as well. "Do you mind if I sit? You too, Gillis. Just there. Tell me what you mean."

"Those men that came last night. Everything they said was true. We know it is Davey's men who have been keeping an eye on things. They never took anything out of turn. Not once. No sheep went missing. We know it was them that kept the duffing outfits off our boundaries. It was like we had a high fence around the whole place. But what the Boss did... humiliating his men like that with a floggin'... he ain't going to take lightly to that Ma'am."

"What do you mean?"

"I mean, Ma'am, that he crossed a line. Davey ain't done anything up to now, but I'm not sure he'll let this pass. Even Callie's Blue said that he's pretty sure there'll be hell to pay now."

"Ted said that?"

"He did Ma'am. I can't talk to the Boss. He'd not be hearing anything on this."

"You did well to come to me. Go and find Ted and bring him to me... regardless of how drunk he is."

Abby called Callie and they went to Cook. Together they pulled out supplies: a dressed sheep, a bag of potatoes, bread and damper, a few kegs of ale, some bags of biscuits. Cook added a half-dozen jars of her bread-and-butter pickles, jam, and a few desert pies. They loaded it onto packhorses, and the stable-hand saddled a couple of mares.

Then she sat on the verandah waiting. Callie was in a fever, pacing back and forth. "Oh, Ma'am I don't know if Gillis will find him. He's got into such a state coming back here. I didn't think he should have, but he said that we needed the money with the little one on its way. I don't know what to do, Ma'am."

Abby calmly took her hand. "Callie, just now we need to wait. Gillis will bring him. If you were not pregnant, I would have you out looking for him as well."

Gillis dragged Ted up towards the verandah; his wet ginger-hair and shirt bore witness to a solid dunking in a water trough. His eyes were bloodshot, and his breath stank. He was tetchy under Gillis' hand until he saw Abby stand and walk down the steps to meet them. He stood up straight and shook himself loose from Gillis's grip. "Damn! Mistress Abby!"

Gillis clipped him under the ear. "Watch your mouth kid. You are talking to a lady."

Ted shook his shoulders. "Did you really want to see me, Mistress Abby? I ain't dragged here for another floggin'?"

"Oh no, Ted, especially when I did all I could, to undo the effects of last time. No, I actually need your help. I want you to be my guide. I need you to take me directly to Davey's camp. No detours and no back routes. Directly there. Understand?"

"But Ma'am. There is a code. We oathed it, proper like... on his Bible. I ain't one to break a sacred oath."

"I know Ted. That is why I have come to you. I have made an oath as well. My pledge is to help. Please don't argue with me. I really have to take these supplies to Mr Davey. Now." There was a firmness in her voice that reminded her of Ruben's recommendation when they were tending to Jay.

Callie quickly pulled him aside. "Ted Horne don't you be giving Mistress Abby any problems now! She has her good reasons. Even if she wanted you to escort her to backend of Hades, I would have you smile, get on your horse, and show her the way. She has only ever been kind and respectful to you and me both!"

"Man! This ain't fair. I can't stand against two women like this."

Gillis nodded grimly. "I reckon you'd have more hope holding out if you were up against the whipping post again, under the threat of your life. We'd best get it done then."

Abby offered a nod of gratitude as Gillis helped her mount up and they rode out. Ted took the lead, Gillis following behind with the pack animals.

They went out passed the dump, and then straight up into the hills. No convoluted trails. They were rounding a narrow track along a high outcrop on the side of the mountain range. Abby paled as she glanced down over the edge and thought the greatest benefit of the blindfold was to spare her vertigo. She felt herself sway and quickly closed her eyes. Her head ached and her wrist throbbed even when she nursed it up out of the way. She took a deep breath and clung firmly to the horn of the saddle with her strong hand and focused her line of sight between her horse's ears. It was then that they encountered Davey coming down the track on foot, followed by his men.

His face was surly, and his green eyes clouded in a storm. He stopped dead when he saw her. She quickly dismounted and walked unsteadily towards him. She stood there, bracing herself against the wall of the mountain pass, as she felt nausea rise from the pain. She took some deep breaths and said nothing.

"You shouldn't come this way. It's risky. What if your horse missteps?"

"I asked Ted to take me directly by the shortest route," she said through her deep breaths.

"And he just did what you said?"

"I was bossy. And I bribed him with bread."

"Huh. And whose life are you saving by your directness this time, Mrs Bates?"

"Yours. Don't do this Ruben. Please. Everything you strive for; all the sacrifices you have made to keep your conscience clear... don't lose all that in a reckless moment of revenge!"

"He has not one fibre of decency! If it was not enough that he would flog his own men without blinking; he flogs and shoots at mine!

He accuses me of being low-life carrion, yet he cowardly abuses you at every turn. He defiles every notion of honour across the board. No one is more deserving of retribution. It is not right!"

"You are correct: it is not right. But I am here. I will honour your respectable alliance in the face of his disregard of it. Don't throw away the path to your dream by what you plan today. Don't become what they accuse you of. Please Ruben. Turn back, so you, at least, will stay on track."

"How can you ask such a thing?"

"Because you have always chosen the better way. Remember what we spoke of... choosing well in the *Meantime*. Don't make this the exception. It will destroy everything you have worked for. The Meantime is still here Ruben... but it won't be forever. Take these supplies. Go back to your camp and allow your men their celebration."

"Mrs Bates, would you also bribe me with bread? Do you think I operate at this basest level of survival? Do you suppose that if you throw me some crusts, I will be content?"

"Survival is a daily matter we all must contend with in some way. This offering I bring you may be simple. Or perhaps it has the makings of a celebration for a group of mates who do well, under difficult circumstances."

"Do well! Do you mock me? I have done no wrong, and yet I am treated like a criminal. He continues to perpetrate all sorts of evil... and he is treated like a king! You make no room for fighting the noble, altruistic fight!"

"I cannot argue that this is the way it should be. But what you are planning, whatever that is... the look in your eye, Ruben Davey, is not noble or altruistic. It is malicious and vengeful. You are above it!"

He stared at her eyes for a time, silenced by her honesty. Eventually he took a deep breath. "Mrs Bates, you make a point. Men! We return to base. Hawk – take the packhorses and unload them; then bring them back by the south track. We will meet you there."

Abby turned to Gillis who had dismounted. "Ted will escort me home with the packhorses." She walked over to him and spoke quietly. "Gillis, please return to your men. Don't mention this to Sorensen – I will talk to him about it later. But do make yourself available to him. He will want to know life goes on." She reached out and touched his arm. "Thank you, Gillis. I am confident your discernment averted tragedy this Shearing."

He nodded, mounted his horse, and turned it towards the homestead. Ruben guided Abby across the pass and stepped back as Ted led her horse by. She gasped, turned her face away, and shuddered in pain holding her wrist.

Ruben looked down at her nursing her hand. "You give Gillis the credit. But I am confident that it was more than his quick thinking that avoided the disaster I scheduled for today."

She shrugged. "Gillis is a good man who works under difficult circumstances. He is honest to a fault and doesn't sugar coat reality. He recognises a bad apple when he sees one, regardless of the toffee coating."

He pointed to her gloved hand, bandages bulking out her wrist. "What happened?"

"I fell... awkwardly. Twisted it as I fell. I didn't break my fall, but my wrist. Heard it crack."

"Did you fall, or did he twist it? Did he push you?"

"Is there a difference? I suspect not. The end result is the same." Her look gave him all the information he needed.

"Come... I will take you over to the south track where we will meet Hawk and Ted. It is the safer route. This way." They walked over rough terrain, and he helped her step around rocks and branches. In some places their route was so concealed, he needed to clear the path forward of forest debris. They paused when they came to a fork in the track where the track widened. Davey stepped aside so Abby could sit on the trunk of a large fallen tree. "Here... take a breather." He took a canteen from around his shoulder and offered her a drink.

She sat, feeling weak from the pain and the strenuous demands of the walk. She murmured her thanks as she drank.

"He breaks your bones and yet you defend him? How is it possible you do that?"

"I don't defend him. His actions speak for themselves. His father told me once that his name, Sorensen... means 'son of the severe'. I thought at the time, nothing could have been more appropriate. He is very much like his father. Old Mr Bates thought it was the cleverest thing: to be identified as severe... cruel even."

"Huh. My name, Ruben, means: 'behold a son'. Just a son. No family baggage to carry. No unattainable virtues to live up to. I like that."

"Ironically, Abigail means "my father is joyful". Actually, he was just desperate. Hence why I am married to a rich man who delights in cruelty. There is no joy in that. Fortunately, my father never got to see what his desperation bought. That is one mercy, I guess."

Ruben looked out into the rocky scrubland of gums and grass-trees with their long dark kangaroo tails pointing up to the sky, and he said nothing for a while. "Abby, thank you. Thank you for coming today. This day would have looked very different if you had not."

She said nothing for a time. She noticed a tantalising glow pulsate in her chest, and she wanted to savour it. Eventually she turned to face him. "Don't forget me, Mr Davey, when your in-between time comes to an end, and your life is what it is destined to be."

His serious eyes glinted, almost as if they glazed over. "Mrs Bates... don't go back. Please. I want you to be safe. I will take you wherever you need to go."

"I must. This is how I understand my marriage vows. Right now... I need to be there. Not for him. For me."

"What he does is a violation of any sort of marriage vows.

"I promised. It is my choice to be there. For now."

He took a deep breath and swallowed. "You are right. It is your choice. But consider what I say. Please." Then he stood to his feet. "Come then. There is still a way to go, and you should not be away from the homestead too long."

⁂

Abby had a bath to rid herself of the smell of horses. As she soaked in the water, scented with lavender oil, and lathered her skin with soap, Ruben's challenge echoed around in her head: *"How can you defend him? Please... don't go back."* Regardless of her assertions, she wondered if she was actually defending his behaviour by her silence. Broken bones? Bruises? Disrespect? It was not the smell of horses that she was trying to wash away, but the shame and contamination that seeped into her pores all over. She was familiar with this sense of smallness, but today, something had expanded in her chest. Today, she had pushed through the pain to feel the glimmer of something she had rarely experienced before. It was when Ruben acknowledged her action that made a difference. What she had done had changed the outcome for something better. This something suggested, that regardless of the appearance of things, it really was worthwhile to speak her mind and not allow intimidation to muffle her voice.

Abby used to think that, as a pretty wife, she would be exempt from Sorenson's rage, but her wrist reminded her that this was not the only broken bone she had carried: ribs, collarbone, and always the bruises. Increasingly, the evidence was that she was not in any way exempt, but in fact, many times she bore the brunt of his moods. She was the master of the cover-up: full skirts and expensive makeup meant no one ever knew. People only saw what they wanted to see, and mostly they were more comfortable being jealous of her prestige. Except Callie. Callie knew. Maybe Gillis. And now Ruben. He guessed straight away. But without pity. And she found that curious. He was angry at the injustice; it was like he included her in the number of his men. He knew the truth, yet he didn't tell her that she brought it on herself, or that if she were a better wife the problem would go away. That thought gave her an additional measure of strength and courage.

But... a hundred 'buts' crowded her mind to taunt her. A hundred voices of advice she had been given over the years. But who would believe her? But who was there to support her? But wasn't a 'nice home' enough? But wasn't it her destiny to take what was dealt to her? But didn't she promise for 'better or worse'? But shouldn't she persevere regardless of whether he hurt her or not?

Who were her allies in this devastating mess? Was Callie? Was Gillis? Was Ruben? She lathered her skin again with lavender soap and lingered on that thought. Her arms ached... not because of the crack in her bone, but they ached to be held and to be loved by a man like Ruben. Perhaps she already did love him. Tears sprinkled her lashes, and she splashed water over her face, as she gasped. It felt like she was drowning.

Then she sat up and checked herself. She was married. To a brute of a man. But married none the less. That would never change. Legally there was not a bishop or a judge in any court of law who would challenge the institution of marriage. It was an unchangeable reality. Just as she supposed that Sorenson's volatile contempt would never change. With him it was just a matter of how far it would fluctuate between suffocating disdain and dangerous cruelty. Regardless of what she held in her heart, she would never have the freedom to be anything else.

Ruben spoke of a world where women could make life supporting choices and speak their mind fearlessly. Perhaps one day, in the far future, there would be such a world where the freedom of divorce was possible, but right now, that was an impossible ideal. The institution of marriage was her prison. She had been forced to marry a man of society. She had married a man of affluence. She knew the rhetoric. That knowledge was a domineering custodial sentence from which she could never escape or pay out the verdict.

But why now? Why had she been given a glimpse of a different world *now*? Why had she been given the glimpse of the vision that Ruben dared to dream of? A world where not everyone was a slave. A world where people could divorce and regain their freedom. A world where everyone had access to liberty. A world where she was respected and esteemed. She sat in the bathwater and determined that even if it was impossible to secure a certificate of divorce, then she could and would, at least be free in the capacity that was available to her.

Today she had held a candle up against the darkness. What she felt in that moment was a mere flicker of what she imagined joy to be. She determined, then, that she would be a person who would light up tapers, and candles, and lanterns, and torches, even bonfires until the dark shadows were expelled! She dressed, bracing her wrist in its pain... and recklessly resolved to be an honourable pyromaniac, joyfully lighting up the darkness in whatever shadowy corner of the world she found herself. She knew just one thing. That corner would be far away from the oppressive empire of Sorenson Bates.

She stepped out of the bath, wrapped a towel around her and felt that she had made the first step to finding her way out of her prison. Her resolution was firm. She was going to do this. She would escape. She would go far away and live a life independent of this.

The sky had clouded over again, and the fire-torches and lanterns were being lit around the shearing shed. Abby looked at them as she drew the curtains. The smoking torches offered a picture of what she had resolved in her heart as they danced against the dark. She turned and lay down on her bed exhausted. She could hear the music and partying continue in full swing. She would tell Sorensen the extent of her interference on the morrow. Or the next. Whenever the moment allowed. In the meantime, everything must seem normal; a shield that pretended life goes on as usual. It must be that way until she could activate her plan to leave.

She closed her eyes, willing herself to sleep. She tossed as rest escaped her and she wished her father had not been a weak man who gambled. He not only squandered her mother's fortune, but he willingly sold his daughter for another. *My father is joyful?* He seemed pleased enough with the bride-price. She scoffed through the dryness of her eyes and the pain tinctures that she had taken, and wished that 'joy' could be inherited, like the fair hair of her mother's; or perhaps the fine china and pretty slippers that were supposed to be enough to make her life fulfilling. Perhaps she could navigate her own dark path to something vaguely like it, or at least a small portion of meaning. And eventually, holding these resolutions firmly in her heart, she dozed off. Restlessly, sleeping, as it were, with one eye open, which is what she always did when Sorensen was home.

She stirred, groggy with sleep, when Callie pulled back the curtains. "Morning Ma'am. Ted told me what you... Oh! Excuse me, Ma'am." Callie quickly put the breakfast tray on a side-table and bobbed a curtsy and left in a hurry as Sorensen stumbled into the room.

Instantly, Abby was awake and hurriedly got out of bed, suppressing her instinct to cry out at the pain shooting through her wrist. She knew that if she could get him to lie down and sleep, perhaps the full extent of the ugliness would be averted. This was familiar: when the snake became a dragon, transformed by booze into a seething ball of rage and violence. And she admitted to herself, in spite of her sleepy resolutions of last night, she was no Saint George, slaying dragons with flaming swords. Her boldness needed to stay alert, covert, and clever, now more than ever. She manoeuvred out of the way, pulled back the sheets. He lunged at her, and he fell on the bed, swearing and slurring in his drunken haze. His boots were muddy and caked in horse manure; his pants were stained with blood, semen, and dirt. That provided its own commentary on what his particular night had been comprised of.

She didn't dare move him or take off his boots. The struggle to do so would disturb him, and her wrist was too sore to manage it by herself anyway. She just left him where he fell, pulled up a light cover and closed the heavy drapes against the morning light. She prayed he would sleep it off. For the most part, things were usually more manageable when the hangover kicked in. She left her breakfast tray on the table and pulled on a gown. Then she went to the kitchen to make another cup of tea for herself using one hand. She sat quietly at the bench looking out the window as the morning light broke through the clouds. Abby wondered how something as beautiful and as fresh as a new morning dawning could be so dark, and bleak, and ominous.

Abby looked out across to the shearing shed that was now, for the most part, still. The musicians were packing up their wagon, and she could see Gillis organising some of his crew. Slowly they were starting the clean-up. The odd seasonal worker was walking away with a swag over their shoulder, trailed by a kelpie or some other mixed mutt who was just as faithful. The end-of-season big-bash was over, and they were all dispersing. Sorensen's mood always became increasingly surly after the show was over. The clouds would gather, and the storm would begin to build-up again, sometimes quite quickly. Davey's delegation had surprised Sorenson and it disoriented his public-face. Normally, the others... the influential others... offered a measure of restraint to keep up appearances among peers. But this time even that was not enough to check him, and he lost control anyway. She braced herself, sipped her cup of tea and wondered how the next few days would play out.

She had a window of armistice while Sorensen slept, and she used the time to attend to some things down at the shearing shed. Abby looked in on Cook and made sure all the china settings from the feast were washed well and repacked in the sawdust of their wooden chests. The wool-classing tables became laundry benches in the clean-up. Mrs Hamill had temporary laundry lines strung up around the shed to cater for the extra tablecloths, towels and sheets from the dinner and the guests that stayed over. A number of additional temporary incinerators were piled with rubbish, and she heard Mrs Hamill bellow out instructions, demanding that they dare not burn anything until the laundry was all brought in. Gillis took Abby over to the shearers' quarters and they checked it over for damage. There was a broken door, a smashed window, and wrecked bunk or two. Someone had even moved a fire-pit inside; there was a scorched hole in the floor, and how the whole building had not erupted in flames she didn't know. She confirmed with the clean-out team that these needed to be fixed before they started on the other maintenance schedules. Abby ensured that Cook send left-overs from the main kitchen down to the workers at the shed for lunch. The work went on at a muted pace contrasting to the frenzy of the past weeks. There were a few snipey scraps between the workers as they nursed their own aching heads. Gillis would pull them apart and put them to work by themselves, creating spaces around their recovery.

When Abby returned to the homestead, she could hear Sorensen's heavy drunken snoring from the hallway. Let sleeping dogs lie. She went instead to a guest room on the lower floor and locked the door before she lay down. The constant throbbing in her wrist was draining. But the most exhausting thing was that constant need to hold her breath, waiting until the next storm raged. That really had her bushed. Her resolution to plan her disappearance was her only reprieve in this oppressive place. When the time was right, she would activate it. Oh, she needed sleep because there were only a few hours before it would start again. Closing her eyes, she tried to imagine she was safe and loved. Deep breaths. And then she tried again, but the exercise was futile for the only place she could imagine such a fantasy, was in the cavern of Ruben Davey. In her desperation to get some sleep, she surrendered to the idea, and found a corner in his cave, back in the recesses and shadows, so she took a holey blanket from his bunk and curled up and went to sleep in the security of believing she was one of his men, and he would fight for her too.

❦

12

Abby startled awake to banging on her door. She sat up, sort of dazed and the relief of sleep quickly swirled away as dread hovered over her. She was in her day dress, and she stood up, smoothed her hair, orientating herself. Her wrist was throbbing again. Instead of opening the door to the obscenities that were being volleyed through the keyhole, she went out the double-doors onto the verandah and came around through the hall. She spoke quietly from the end of the hallway as Sorensen continued to thump on the door of the guest room. "Were you looking for me?" He didn't hear. "Sorensen! Are you looking for me?"

His hand stood suspended as he went to thump the door-frame again and a strange look passed over his face. He paused for just a moment as if he was perplexed. But he pushed it aside and turned to her with a frown and swore. "Obviously! I need a bath and food. That tray is dead cold! Goodness woman, for one who claims such skill in managing a household, your incompetence is mind-blowing! Draw me a bath, and have some decent food brought to me!"

Nothing but demands punctuated with lurid swearing. "Very well. I will see to it right away." She turned to go. Then she paused and turned back. "Sorensen. I sent some of the leftover goods up to Davey's camp. He was on a mission for revenge after the mistreatment of his men. His anger has been way-laid and he is placated for now. Although I doubt very much, he will show any interest in protecting your mobs of sheep next season."

Sorensen gaped at her in shock. He shook his head again as if he couldn't quite hear what she had said. He scratched his head and his groin in a confused sort of daze. Suddenly he activated. He bounded towards her like a lumbering monster, in the temper of the fabled "hairy-man" yowies, fuming his rage in horrible guttural bellows.

He was on her in a moment. Abby, normally alert to the unexpected, was completely sideswiped by the momentum of his bulk. He flung her along the hallway like a rag doll, and pursued her, standing over her in his crazed fury. He lifted his big hands in his frenzy, the veins on his neck popping-out as his face washed beetroot-red. Suddenly, the dragon in full ferocity, froze. His face contorted, and he collapsed on top of her. It was like someone had cut the marionette strings that moved his body, and his body went flaccid, weighted like wet canvas.

Abby shrieked as he pinned her, the wind knocked out of her slight frame. She gasped and tried to roll him off her chest, but his bulk was too much against her bone-tender wrist. She gasped and tried to call for help but her voice scarcely registered. With her good arm she restlessly banged the polished floorboards and squeaked, again and again.

It was forever before she heard footsteps, and then Mrs Hamill's voice cried above her. "Oh, my goodness Mr Bates! Mistress Abby! Help! Somebody, help me!" She levered him onto his side and quickly pulled Abby to her feet. "Ma'am! Are ye okay? What happened? Help! Somebody, help!"

Suddenly the homestead, sleepy in recovery, was activated. Every attendant and workman appeared, buzzing in their shock. Abby crouched against the hallway wall gasping in shock. Breathlessly she tried to focus. "Put Mr Bates into bed and get Gillis to send someone for the doctor." He lay still on the floor, but even then, it did not occur to Abby that this was anything other than the effects of a bad hangover. "He just needs some more rest."

Mrs Hamill dispatched Callie to fetch Gillis. A couple of men brought in an old door, and they used it to stretcher him into the bedroom. They removed his boots and brushed off the soiled fragments that littered the sheets as they lifted him onto the mattress and then rolled his bulk off the platform. She positioned him on pillows and pulled up the covers as his lids twitched erratically and drool pooled from his mouth. She shook her head unsympathetically and then went to the washstand and poured some water into the basin. As she started to wash his face, she summarised to Gillis what the messenger needed to tell the doctor when he rode into town to fetch him.

⁂

Doctor Sanders strapped his bag closed. "Mrs Bates, how did you find him? How long had he been like this?"

"Oh. I um... Well, he came in late after... well he had been drinking all night, so he went straight to bed. He is usually fine when he sleeps it off. When he woke up, he was looking for me. I called out but when he came towards me, he just sort-of collapsed. I think I knocked my head because I don't remember much after that. It seemed a long time".

Mrs Hamill positioned a fresh jug of water. "Excuse me, Doctor. I saw the whole thing. Hardly took a moment from when he fell to when we called the men to help put him in bed."

Abby turned away. "It felt like forever."

"Mrs Bates? I fear it may not make any difference. This is not a common hangover as you suppose. This is an apoplexy turn. People

77

don't recover from an episode like this. You need to prepare for the worst. He may not recover at all." He looked at her sympathetically.

Abby nodded soberly. When Dr Sanders said, '*he may not recover*', she suspected he actually meant there was no hope Sorenson would do anything other than be back on his feet, in full swing, within the week. She dared not expect anything less... or more. Old Mr Bates had such an episode... and she nursed him for another two and a half years. She remembered after his last episode, his body had been warm, but it was deadweight, like dressed lumps of meat. When it came to Sorensen her compassion was bone dry. She wiped his face again, just for something to do. And resigned herself again, to the harsh reality that this life was her lot. Her plans for freedom had collapsed, crushed like the weight falling on her in the hallway. How like Sorensen: to dominate and sabotage her last vestige of hope.

Sorensen moved and slurred his words agitatedly. The doctor opened his bag again. "If you can get him to swallow, give some of this draught. It may help to calm him. Keeping him as comfortable as possible is the best you can hope for."

So that was what Abby did. She kept him as comfortable as she could. He could not swallow, but she dripped the elixir into his mouth with the optimism that some would trickle down his throat. He stirred sometimes in an agitated restless sleep. At other times he was so still, and his breathing so shallow, she thought it was over. Night after night she tended him. She had the men move a spare bunk into the room and she stayed there with him. There was something so completely tragic by his incapacitation, and yet even this hardly moved her with sympathy. It was not like she thought he deserved it. No one deserved this. It was unpleasant and cruel, just like the reality of her life. And now for this time, it was his reality too. How ironic that he was dying in the same way he had forced her to live... trapped and unable to move. It had been many years since she tended Old Mr Bates like this, yet she was calm in the task. And she stole snatches of sleep through her vigil of nursing him.

Gillis came into the room. "Ma'am? Do you have to attend to every duty yourself?"

"That I do, Gillis. I am his wife."

"But he weren't that good a husband."

"I do it... not because he deserves it, but because I believe in the dignity of each of us. This is about the type of person I am... not who he is or was."

"But you are doing all of this with a busted wrist. It ain't right. There are house staff who can help."

"Of course. I have help when I need it..." She paused and then turned to him. "Gillis? Doctor Sanders believes Sorensen will not recover. I need you to be aware... if... when... that happens, it is incumbent of me to notify Sorenson's legal firm. I cannot guarantee what changes will or will not be made."

"Yes, Ma'am I know. Well, please let me or Mrs Hamill know if you need someone to help you in the meantime."

She jolted when he said it. *Meantime?* But when she looked up from where she was rubbing lanolin into his dry rough hands Gillis had already turned to leave. "Thank you, Gillis. Thank you. I will."

On the fortnight it was over. She laid her head on the bed beside his body, exhausted. Tears of relief came in gasps, as the smell of death hovered in the room and quietly evaporated. Slowly she allowed the elation of emancipation to flood through her as her tears washed her cheeks.

Callie guided her gently back to the guest room frowning. Did she really grieve him after all he had done? The other staff watched, and shook their heads, and thought it was beautiful that she loved him so much; and sighed at the tragedy that she was to be a widow so young.

⁓⁓⁓❦⁓⁓⁓

13

Abby sat in her black dress and pulled back her veil and removed her hatpins. She took off her bonnet and unpinned her veil folding it up separately. She sat in the library; the door locked against the rest of the house and the curtains to the verandah open. A cup of tea sat on the tray before her. For just a moment she needed to get away from the prying eyes of Sorenson's relatives, and the gathering volt of vultures that were now circling the Bates' Empire. It was ironic that she had overheard servants recount Sorensen's Shearer's Feast vent, accusing Ruben with that very same metaphor: vultures. It fitted better here. She opened the doors onto the verandah and let some of the air breeze through. She looked at the shelves of books and felt a twinge of sadness that she had to say goodbye. She sighed. Who would ever have thought that she would miss this symbol of her uninformed life here with Sorensen?

She heard the French doors latch and the curtains draw. She jolted and turned around. "Oh! Ruben..."

"You are looking very much the grieving widow, Mrs Bates. I am sorry for your loss." He soberly waited for her to take her seat and sat opposite her. His clothes were clean and laundered. He didn't look any different from all the other mourners dressed in black who were traversing her life.

"I grieve the good things that were part of my life here. It all changes now. Widowhood is not just mourning a husband. I have many friends who have stood by me here... and now I have to say goodbye to them also."

"Bates was a wealthy man. Does this not make you a wealthy widow?"

"Well... Sorenson has an adult son, Rupert, from his first marriage. And any number of illegitimate children, who will no doubt now make their move to be included in some way. Essentially it means that this fat lamb pie has many pieces that numerous people will be fighting over for their serve. No doubt Sorensen organised it so that it will be left free and clear to Rupert as his legitimate heir, and the others will not get what they hope for. But still, it is predictable they will try. I imagine the squabbling will go on for some time. I have no expectation that any of this will include me. They are already moving in and moving on."

"Did you give your life to this man, not to be considered?"

"Consideration hasn't been my lot until now. This is not new. I am not shocked."

"So what? You get nothing?"

"I get my life back. That is everything."

"Hmm." He sat there thoughtfully. "Mrs Bates..."

"Ruben I am no longer married to him. The *'Til Death do us part'* clause means I am released, even from his name. Please call be Abby."

"Okay. Abby... I..." His voice faulted and he cleared his throat, his green eyes unreadable. "You said that you wished me to remember you when I step into my future. I promised I would but..." He swallowed hard and looked at his hands.

"Would you abandon me also, Ruben?" She stood up abruptly and stared him down. Her life was unravelling, and it seemed this last thread of hope snapped before her eyes. "Oh! I am so gullible! You find out I do not inherit, and you lose all interest? I truly believed all your rhetoric for a better world, and an idealism so grand... but it seems all you wanted was to be included in this scavenger fight too! Goodness! I disgust even myself!" She turned away and did not see the raw shock on his face. She felt a dark cloud of uncertainty smothering her. "I think you should leave before I call, and have you arrested."

He frowned then. "Arrested? For offering my condolences?"

"You forget that you are a wanted man, Ruben."

"You forget that there are no arrest warrants. Those incentives are a private matter to enhance their opportunity for gathering dirt. They cannot even call me a person of legal interest. Come Abby. You haven't bought into that? You know me!"

She turned back and shook her head. "I thought I did... but I think what I bought into was a charming charade – lock, stock, and barrel. That's all I know! You'd better go."

"Abby..." He moved towards her, and she backed away.

"Don't! Just don't." Her eyes filled with tears that blurred her sight, as her hand found the doorknob behind her back, and she fled to guestroom. The master bedroom had already been commandeered by Rupert and his pregnant wife. Now she was delegated to the status of 'visitor' in her own home. She sat on the bed and allowed her tears to flow. "No! This can't be real. His friendship was life to me." She sobbed into her pillow and felt the stress of these last weeks drain the last of her steadfastness. She had no idea what life would look like now. Her one hope had been that he would be there to catch her fall. Ruben hadn't pushed her like Sorensen, but he had stepped back and watched her crash. She was all alone.

❧❧❧

14

Ruben sat against the trunk of a tree and looked out over the valley. He considered the small tinder-box size buildings scattered along the valley floor. He pictured Redwood Park in his mind... the library, the verandah, Abby walking in her garden. He had gone there. He could not stay away. Knowing her circumstances were changed, it was as impossible to stay silent as it was to stay distant. He had never intended to declare his love, but as soon as he saw her, he had started down that track without even realising it. And yet... yet... he shook his head bewildered. He could not comprehend how that encounter had turned on its head so abruptly.

He sighed. He had found himself so completely in love with an unavailable woman. Married. Committed and unreachable, albeit behind the wall of a man who was despicable in every aspect of his life. Ruben knew the moral ground. He had guarded his words; he had guarded his conversation; he had guarded his manner. He had guarded everything... except staying away. The incident with Jay had caused such turmoil. Ruben had battled and tossed and eventually rationalised his insistence she attend Jay with her nursing skill. As he sat looking over the valley, watching the sun dip low towards a hazy rust-red horizon, he sighed again. He had been so strict around his choice of language. Yet, if he was honest, it wasn't so much his concern for Jay that motivated him, but his weakness. He had been unable to stay away. So, he had identified his Achille's heel. He had discovered his vulnerability: he could not endure staying away.

Was her rejection divine retribution? Was this his punishment for stepping so close to that moral line, even though he never crossed it? He defended his behaviour, on the basis he had not actually committed any crime, but his conscience insisted he walked too close to the line. He had re-enacted in his mind, the sitting of a moral court, and even then, they could not convict him. And when he had finally snapped and was going to avenge her and his men, she stepped in and demanded he see sense. But was that enough for God? Was God a Divinity who dealt out reprisal for being fallible and human? Would he be condemned for feeling what was impossible for him not to feel?

He had held himself in check when every fibre of his being was screaming otherwise. He had submitted himself to a personal torment, no matter how much he ached to rescue her and protect her and hold her. The woman was insanely exceptional, and he was not just considering her slight figure and bewitching eyes. Her regard and courage and boldness demanded his respect. Her forbearance under Bates' flagrant disregard for the sacredness of marriage, had his total admiration. When Abby had told him that she was sold like a breeding ewe to pay out her father's debts, he felt his anger flash hot at the injustice. She deserved more. She deserved to be loved. She deserved him. But she had shut him out before he could voice that possibility.

He paused and then quickly stood upright. He saw the glint of mirror flashing in the evening sunlight from the dump site. Was it possible? Few knew the signal. He could not see who was there from this distance, and caution demanded he take care.

⁕

Dusk was rapidly falling as he reached the tree line. He saw her pacing, backwards and forwards. He followed the cover of evening shadows and when she turned back around again in her pacing he was leaning against a tree, watching her carefully. Why had she come?

When they last spoke, he was so very repulsive to her. But now she was here... alone. He had to hear what she had to say.

She was wringing her hands and did not even look up before she turned again, pacing back along the temporary circuit she had set herself. Finally, he tipped his hat, and she caught the movement and froze. "Oh. You have finally come," she said curtly.

He shrugged. Last time his words condemned him, even before he had been able to state his case. He didn't want to make another false move like that. She came and stood before him, her eyes searching his face.

"Dickens said you wanted to speak with me. I thought perhaps you had changed your mind and would not come. I did not like that we left on poor terms, and I wanted..." She stopped and swallowed awkwardly.

Ruben handed her a flask from his shoulder, and she took a drink. His heart racing. "Dickens delivered my message?" Nothing in his face suggested that he had not assigned Dickens with any such dispatch.

"He didn't ambush me like last time, but he was very definite." She shrugged. "So here I am. Summoned again. But I have something I wish to say first."

He offered nothing more than a speculative, "Oh?"

She closed her eyes and took a breath. "I wanted you to know that I have regarded our companionship well, and I feel disappointed that you would abandon our friendship so abruptly."

"Abandon you? You told me to leave."

She turned and studied his face. "As soon as you discovered I was impoverished as a widow dependant entirely on the good-will of my stepson, you were unable to..." She stopped, glaring. He made no move or attempt to speak. "Do you have nothing to say in the defence of this inexcusable position? The evidence is not looking respectable for you Mr Davey." He had used those same words against herself once.

"You are right. The evidence does seem stacked against me... but I feel that I was not able to state my entire case. The delivery of my position was cut short. I would petition leave to finish presenting my entire defence... your Honour," he said with a wry grin.

She stood still and nodded.

"What I would say..." he cleared his throat and gathered his thoughts. "I said I would give you all consideration when my name is cleared. But my hesitation is not due to the diminished degree of my regard for you. My concerns are of a practical nature. What I mean is... I am still living as a vagabond in the hills. I haven't started the legal process of restoring my reputation or my place in society. The *Meantime* is still here for me... and I don't know for how long this will go on for. I... I am not sure that I can..." He swallowed hard and held up his hand as the line of her lips went thin and she started to interject once more. "Abby, I don't think I can wait. I don't want to wait that long."

"What do you mean? Are you not going to pursue your legal recourse?"

"I will pursue it of course, but the outcome is uncertain. What if my *Meantime* is all I ever experience until eternity? How can I wait out for some distant day that may never come? But then, even if I don't want to wait, how can I ask, or expect, someone to follow me into such an unknown?"

"Your men do it. You expect it of them."

"But they are displaced and disillusioned. My offer is just a little better than the hell they come from. It doesn't make it a good option, just an improved one. The bar is set too low for you."

She moved away and stood by the rusted metal frame of an old plough. "I understand that hell too. Your little cave has been a refuge for me. Not because you can't improve your décor, but because *you* are there. You Ruben, *you* are better than the hell where I have lived."

He came over and stood before her. Expectation thoughtfully lit his eyes as he searched her face. "Could you leave your lavish comforts, to live with me in this *Meantime*? Could it be possible I might presume that of you?"

"No. You cannot *presume* it..." She looked up into his eyes, and they flickered again with dread of what he didn't want to hear. "But Ruben, you can *ask* it of me. But please, this is not the place to use your courtroom lawyering on me to build a logical case. I am not talking to a lawyer here. I am talking with you."

"What would you have me say?"

"Say what is on your heart."

"You would have me say that I am blown away by your compassion and grace and style and loveliness and sense? Would I say that I cannot understand how you have nurtured, not just the beauty of your lovely face, but of your soul, in a place that is as barren as the deserts of the inland? And yet you have. And I find myself so deeply in love it terrifies me that I will never live in the shadow of your affection. What if my feelings may never be reciprocated? Because I cannot deny that my Meantime is a meagre unpleasant reality, and you deserve so much more."

"Deeply in love? How can I possibly deserve more than that?"

"I do love you... with every fibre of my being. Waves of it have been dumping me upside down ever since you first traversed my life uninvited. You were untouchable then, and I have restrained my hope and endeavoured to keep my distance... none too successfully I acknowledge. But Abby, you have moved me and changed me, even from a distance."

"I am changed too. You have showed me a different sort of strength. A strength that is good and noble and humble, and yet, much more powerful than the dominance and abuses I have lived with. It is overwhelming for me to think this is even imaginable. You dream the magnificent again, Mr Davey. It hardly seems possible."

And the tears that washed her face as he gathered her into his arms tasted of joy.

15

Abby sat down at a table in the corner of the teahouse and looked through the dingy glass windowpane and frowned. Greystone. Grey said it all. It was a telling name for a community. Her altruistic ambitions had been about living uncomplaining in the paucity of mountain caves when they married; but now that dream seemed to melt under the stench of sewage that wafted up from the street every morning. Moving out of Redwood Park had been no real sacrifice, but what she had moved *into* was still sending shockwaves through her. She opened her purse and dabbed a little more lavender water on her neck. The rooms they had rented were meagre, and the furniture was sparse. Not that she minded that particularly. The caverns in the hills barely had furniture... but they didn't smell. The clean mountain air that washed each morning in rising mist, just now, were closer to heaven.

Life was strange in this in-between place. There was a cloak of secrecy that constantly hovered around their plans. She was trying very hard to understand why it had to be this way, the practical matters of affordability aside, waiting for the mourning period to pass, until they could officially become betrothed, seemed like a dark tunnel that would never end. Any type of distraction that allowed her to get out of their rooms, to be honest, was a relief. She was delighted when Ruben suggested they met in this shabby corner of a teahouse, especially because it was far enough away to offer a little relief from the revolting smell of Greystone gutters.

Ruben put his coat over the back of his chair and sat down to pour his tea that had been steeping too long. He seemed thoughtful, almost preoccupied as he stirred his cup and tried to drown some persistently floating tealeaves with the bent teaspoon he had attempted to straighten. He took a drink, paused, and then put down his cup as if he had come to a particular resolution. "Abby, what do you think about betraying someone who may someday be your betrothed?"

"What? No, I would never! You know I would not."

"But... hear me out... what if you could? There is a lucrative reward pending for persons with information. You have a significant amount of information. It is worth money."

"Your men have not abused that knowledge; why would I?"

"To fund my defence. As noble that this puritan, non-mercenary, hermit life is... it doesn't provide for the necessities to engage the British legal system... even in an outpost colony. Regardless of my reputation I'm not going to start holding-up stagecoaches. It is not my style."

"You *want* me to do this?"

"They have accused me without grounds. They have refused to pay out the partnership agreement. I appreciate the irony that they could fund the expenses required to clear my name."

"Ruben, I have a number of pieces of jewellery. Perhaps it is fortunate that it suited Sorenson to have his wife adorned ostentatiously. Those pieces are part of what I can legitimately say were chattels from my marriage. With the right brokers, they could bring in a substantial amount."

"They are yours. But this is not just about my exoneration. I want to use the reward to start a seed-fund for our men as well."

"A seed-fund?"

"Seed: an initial amount they can plant and grow to invest for the next part of their lives. This time in the hills is a transition place for them to prepare... a margin to help them get back on their feet. We need money for that. This cannot be their forever plan either."

"I think you underestimate their willingness to follow you through all sorts of circumstances. I suspect their devotion is not just a stepping-stone to future stability."

"I think of it as a railway platform to somewhere else. I have never suggested this situation to be anything more."

She looked at him and saw he sincerely believed his assertions. "Can you be so certain that they carry this arrangement so loosely? Each one marched with you bent on revenge, just because you suggested it. Don't underestimate your influence here, Ruben."

"Influence I am okay with. But that is all it is."

She shook her head and doubted he appreciated the intensity of their allegiance. She understood it because it was becoming her devotion too. What would she do, just because he suggested it? "This disclosure, do you seriously want me to do this? How is it helpful to have you arrested, in gaol, and closer to a noose?"

"I've studied the reward notice." He reached into his jacket and pulled out a folded sheet and spread it on the table between them. "They are paying for information... not my capture. That is what we need to contract. On the basis of this technicality, we will not break the intent of their reward."

⁂

Abby walked up the stairs into the offices of Crosby and Moore that overlooked the main street. She noted the shingle on the street had been recently repainted and no longer read Crosby, *Davey,* and Moore. She was dressed in her mourning black and took the seat that was offered to her with a nod.

"It is a pleasure to see you again, Mrs Bates. Our condolences for your loss."

She adjusted her veil and didn't correct either the myth of her sorrow, or the pleasure of this meeting. "Many things have changed for me, Mr Crosby."

He nodded solemnly. Abby sighed and sat still for a time. Then she held up her hand and took off her glove. Her left hand held just one plain band on her finger. "Do you see this cheap band, Mr Crosby? Do you know what it means?"

"It is the ring of widowhood. How distraught you must be, Mrs Bates."

"Sorenson was generous in bestowing jewellery. Some of those pieces were fashionable. But now my life has changed. It has been incumbent of me to hock these symbols of our marriage to resource my altered circumstances."

"Mr Bates, God rest his soul, was a very rich man."

"Come, Mr Crosby, you were his solicitor. Your firm represents Rupert. You know I don't see that money."

"You still wear a band. You are young; you could remarry."

"It is barely two months since Sorensen passed. It would be unseemly to consider such a thing before the period of mourning is past. Besides, marriage is not the only means of survival, Mr Crosby. There are other ways to provide a living."

He took a drink of water and looked confused. She seemed cold. Calculating. This was not the cordial, accommodating Mrs Sorensen Bates that he was familiar with. Perhaps living in the frost had turned her heart stone cold. Who could blame her?

"I also wear this ring because I am not yet ready to flaunt my eligibility, Mr Crosby. In fact, I still feel very much committed." She reiterated in her mind the reasons she was engaging in this charade.

"Oh of course, Mrs Bates. Of course, you do."

"Which brings me to my dilemma. A few pieces of jewellery... even nice pieces with quality gemstones... well, they have only limited value at a pawn-brokers. If I am not going to sell my life in wedlock to another man to survive, I need to source other income. At least for a time." She coughed delicately. His eyes lit up, and she closed her lids behind her widow's veil as she felt his eyes run over her figure. She felt nauseous reflux burn the back of her throat at the obvious turn of his thoughts. She pulled out a sheet of paper printed with the header: *Reward for Information*. She placed it on his desk. "I have information."

"Oh." He cleared his throat awkwardly. "I heard you were sympathetic to this reprobate's cause. Bates denied any connection of course."

"Perhaps what you heard was not without grounds. Yet sympathy is easy when you have buttered bread and new dresses at your disposal. Reality does not always lend itself so magnanimously to a well-meaning cause."

"Hmm." He took another drink, cleared his throat again and did his best to look indifferent.

Abby noted a hungry look in his eye. No, he was not disinterested, no matter how much he coughed. "Mr Crosby, Rupert is not inclined to support his stepmother. I am an imposition and no longer welcome in a place that has been my home for many years." That was a truthful assertion. She tapped the sheet of paper on his desk.

"What would you really pay for this information? *'Up to...'* is a little vague."

"We've had nothing substantial come to light at this point. There is no expectation that what you could offer would be different."

Abby sat up, and leaned forward, and spoke quietly. "I know where his lair is. I paid off his men after that shearing debacle. You were at the Shearer's Feast. You heard what they wanted. I took them the rations they demanded. I paid their ransom, and now it is my turn. I can lead you directly to his hideout. Sorensen's men trusted them. I've asked around. They still hide there."

Crosby took a drink and then cleared his throat... again.

"Mr Crosby, this renegade splattered shame over the professional reputation of your firm. People are still talking about it. Your silent passivity is allowing his outrageous behaviour to go unchallenged." She paused and picked up the paper. "I am sorry, Mr Crosby, for wasting your time."

"Well, Mrs Bates, the mercenary look is as different on you as your mourning weeds. You have taken me quite by surprise. I will allow one thing: our lack of useful leads has been unfortunate."

"Don't give up yet, Mr Crosby. Your showdown with that man is within your reach. What do you give me to escort you to his lair? I have expenses..."

"Mrs Bates, we would require proof of your commitment to deliver."

"I guarantee, Mr Crosby, I am committed to seeing this money. Half now, and half when I guide you into his camp."

"That is entirely unreasonable: ten percent is more than generous. I will have to speak to my partner."

She stood up and handed over a slip of paper. The hungry look intensified. She suspected that this was the first solid lead they had received in a while. She truly felt like Judas, selling information when even a needy community refused to do it. Even the notorious Ned Kelly had not been sold out by his neighbours. The Law could not find him. "I deal directly with you and your partner. No third parties. I am staying at this hotel. It is cheap but it is typical of what my life now is. I vacate at midday tomorrow, so you will need to let me know of your decision before then. I will come back to collect the part payment if you are agreeable to these terms."

Mr Crosby watched through the window as she left and walked down the street. Then he called his assistant and instructed him to follow the widow to see if she was indeed checked in at the Ram's Head Inn. He was to follow up with both the local pawnbrokers to see if any jewellery items had recently been deposited by a Mrs Abigail Bates.

16

Abby restlessly paced around the narrow bed and the grubby upholstered chair. It seemed an entirely risky game. But she reminded herself of the calm look in Ruben's eyes as he laid out their strategy. She took a deep breath. At a quarter past eleven, a message was delivered to her door. They had accepted her offer, and part-payment was awaiting her collection.

She clutched her bag as they indicated for her to be seated. Moore had several rough looking men standing silently along the wall. They reminded her of a muster of crows lined up on a fence rail eyeing off the carcass of a dead sheep.

"Who are these men? I said no third parties."

"Merely associates, Ma'am. Crosby tells me you can show us where this man hides." He pushed over a portion of their payment.

"My word is true," she murmured, counting the money. "And the remaining part?"

"Obviously we can't pay until our deal is delivered in full."

"A verbal agreement is as good as gossip. At least give me a statement of confidence in writing that when I show you his haunt I will be paid. The rest is up to you."

Abby reached into her purse and pulled out a scribbled note on low quality yellowed paper, with a duplicate. She put them on the desk. Crosby raised his brow. "You've already signed it. You come prepared Mrs Bates."

"This is the best I could do under the circumstances. Mr Bates is no longer my intermediary. I have no intention of having you charge me for draughting up an official document. Even if it is not polished, it says what it means. I won't waste your time." She took out her kerchief and smothered a humiliating sniffle.

Crosby looked at it with a smirk. Mrs Bates would not have the savoir-faire to pursue the terms of any agreement. He shrugged and signed it, including the receipted amount of the deposit.

She picked up the sheet and handed it to Mr Moore who was standing by the window. "Would you counter sign it, Sir?" she asked with a whimper. He shrugged, signed, and dated it with a condescending flourish. She tucked it in her purse with the money and handed Crosby the copy. "I feel entirely reassured that as partners you are in agreement. Well then, Gentlemen, let us be on our way; no need to delay."

As she walked out of the office, she bumped into a passer-by. She apologised profusely, quickly passing the package of the payment into Dickens' hands, including the note of surety.

She climbed up into the carriage, hugged her purse tightly and looked out the window benignly. Going out to Redwood Park station was timed with one of Rupert's trips away. It was hot and generally unpleasant, and she kept her thoughts to herself. She fanned her face with her eyes closed, nodding off in rhythm to the rocking motion, as she listened to the men's speculation. At the homestead, she presented herself to Gillis, who provided her group with horses. They mounted up and rode out towards the boundary dump. Gillis agreed to come as her chaperone, as she trusted him. They tethered the horses in the shade and walked towards the foothills leading to the track up the mountain. She turned around and paused. "Gentlemen? Are you coming?"

"We are walking? Up there?"

"Yes, and if we don't get started, we will be caught in the dark. It is quite a way."

They gathered their wits and loosened their cravats. To be outdone by a woman seemed entirely unreasonable.

Abby walked, and paused, and occasionally she looked uncertain. Ruben had put clear markers for her to follow, which she knocked out of the way as she passed. Her fluster was convincing, if not real at some points. She had brought with her an old pillowcase that she ripped into strips and tied a band to a branch every so often, to mark the track back. "There are no clear paths, most of these are just kangaroo tracks. My guide was the husband of my maid." She tied another strip of fabric. "The trip back down will be quicker because I have marked the path clearly." She feigned fear, as they edged along the mountainside, and sat exhausted on a rock taking a long drink from her water canteen. "I think we are close now," she said as they turned along a bend in the track, and it opened out onto the camp. The fireplace was cold, the canvas curtains on the doors were torn, their makeshift furniture overturned and some of it smashed.

Abby stood there confused. "I don't understand. My informant said they still were still active in the district."

Crosby looked around. "You have brought us on a wild goose chase!"

"Gentlemen, this is where I handed over the goods. See, that is one of our coopered barrels." She pointed to the Redwood insignia branded into the wood. She barged over to Ruben's cave and walked inside. Everything that indicated recent occupation was gone. The table, stool and bunk remained, stripped and bare. She stormed around frustrated. "This is his place! How else would I know where to bring you?"

Just then she saw one of her earrings in the dust, and she quickly covered it with her boot. She knelt down to retie her laces and smuggled it into the lining of her bodice. Then she pointed out a screwed-up piece of paper under the table before she stood up. Moore reached over and picked it up. He flattened it out on the table. It looked like a torn-out diary entry. One side referred to the humiliation of the Shearer's Feast. It was dated and signed. The next entry had a number of simple mistakes that were carelessly crossed out; the lettering was wonky; and the grammar was poor; the language sounded common as if the author was writing under the influence. It referred to the peace offering brought by Mrs Bates, and the clumsy construction of the entry offered a simple explanation as to why the page was discarded. As Moore handed the page to his associates, he traced the carved initials etched into the timber of the table. Ruben had coloured his name with charcoal to make it seem less like a recent addition. They stared at it. "It seems, Mrs Bates, this was his camp after all. It is unfortunate that he is no longer here. This voids our contract of course. We cannot pay on what was not delivered."

She looked scandalised and objected loudly. "I risk everything to bring you up into these inhospitable mountains, and you simply say you do not need to pay? It is as I feared."

"You said so yourself, Mrs Bates, your life has changed. Perhaps you will need to find other ways to finance your inclination for a comfortable lifestyle," said Crosby with a leer. Moore came over and grabbed the satchel that was slung across her shoulder, breaking the strap.

Gillis stepped forward. "Now hang on..."

One of Crosby's brutes knocked his jaw with the butt of his rifle and knocked him to the ground. When Gillis struggled to his feet, he was pinned back and cautioned off with the rifle. Moore tipped her bag out over the table. There was a handkerchief, a scarf, a notebook, a wrapped piece of bread, a small vial of perfume, some lotion and smelling salts. There was no envelope with the money they had given her, nor the note of surety. She gasped. "The envelope! Where is my money? Did you take it from me on the trip here?"

Moore shrugged, and then a smile dawned on his face. "Aah... when we came out of the office, a scruffy man bumped into you on the street, just before you got up into the carriage. I would say, Mrs Bates, that you are the victim of a common pick-pocket."

"I am robbed? No! Did *you* arrange to have him to take my reward?"

"Careful, Mrs Bates. You are becoming quite paranoid in your widowhood. Perhaps this is the natural course of justice." He shrugged and smiled. "You have not delivered, so now there is no need for us to deliver either." There was a look in his eye that reminded her of Sorensen.

"But I *have* delivered, just as we agreed. You still owe me the remaining portion of our agreement. You signed the paper stating *these* were our terms!" She sounded quite panicked.

Moore scratched through the contents of her purse. "Huh. I see no evidence of any such an agreement. I would reiterate that there is nothing to pay."

"But you signed it! *You* even counter signed it! You kept a copy. Sorensen used your firm for his business. He trusted you. How can you turn against me so?"

"We have no further business with Mr Bates now. He owes us nothing. God rest his soul".

Gillis struggled to release himself from their grip as Crosby stepped forward. "Unless there *is* another way that you would earn your money, Mrs Bates?"

Their thoughts had flipped, and Abby was genuinely uneasy. "I will make my own way back!" she said quickly as she rushed outside.

Two others stood outside in the clearing and barred her escape down the track. "Not sure you can leave yet, Ma'am," they said, holding her arms.

"No, we are not done! We will not suffer loss... to you, or this renegade bushranger," said Moore emphatically.

"Your loss? You are the ones who have refused to pay."

Crosby came up close to her and stared at her cleavage with an ugly suggestion in his eye. "Then you will be lost in the mountains. It is an unfortunate story around these parts."

Abby panicked as they jostled her roughly. She struggled and they pulled at her bodice. Suddenly a gun report split the air. They stopped, momentarily stunned. Ruben barged in on his horse, and they fell back as he grabbed her. Abby's eyes were desperate, fighting his restraining hold as he roughly slung her over the saddle in a single move. Ruben reigned his horse around and he turned in his saddle. "Gentlemen! Is this the way you protect your informants?" he shouted. "You needn't worry, I'll take it from here!" He dug in his heels and spurred his horse on, and they disappeared through the scrub.

The men stood immobilised for a moment until one of the men started to follow. Moore reined him in. "Don't. This solves everything. Finally, we have a charge that will stick: unlawful abduction. The law can do the chasing now."

Ruben reined in his horse. Abby shook herself loose and slid off the horse. "Ruben! You promised you would stay away!"

Ruben dismounted beside her. "There is no way I was *not* going to have surveillance on this situation, beginning to end."

She took a shuddering breath and nodded. She was grateful. Setting up the ruse had been exhilarating. But that... that was too real!

"The kidnapping explains your disappearance." He kissed her lightly. "They will follow your trail markers down the hill. We to have wait until they are beyond the narrow pass on the ravine."

"Ruben, my distress is not playacting. Can't we just let them be? Why don't we go somewhere else? Jump that ship to Europe that it was rumoured you stowed away on. We could be married straight away."

"Tempting as that is, first let us make their return to our little camp inconvenient in case that is on their mind."

"But..."

"*But* now we have money to start fighting our way out of this mess. Thank you. You have done well."

They watched the men trail back down the mountain, following Abby's beaconed markers of white linen strips. As they finally edged across the narrow track around the ravine, Ruben signalled with a single report from his pistol. Hawk executed a well-aimed blow of his axe, slicing through some sisal rope that was holding a bundle of large, felled trees back like a dam wall suspended above the pass. The tree trunks broke free, sheering down the mountain-side in a rush. The men retreated, swearing, and shaken, as the small narrow path around the mountain outcrop disappeared in their wake, leaving them on the station-side of the mountain track.

They watched until the crashing of the timber stilled in the ravine below. Gillis took the lead as their guide, and they turned back along the track towards the homestead.

They were gone. Ruben looked down at Abby and paused before he kissed her. "Well, Mrs Bates, you are still courageous and fearless in the face of all sorts of challenges," he said softly.

"I've heard it said that courage is not fear-*less*, without fear... but moving forward through the horror of fear anyway. You show courage too."

"I have another fear I have alluded to many times. And I will not be content until I have addressed it." He dropped to his knee. "I am in love more than ever. Please Abby, will you be my wife? Even in the meantime?"

She looked around at the rough mountain rocks, and trees, and at this roughly dressed man speaking so gently. She took his bearded face in her hands. "I would gladly swap my widow-band for your ring."

"This is not as flashy as your previous one," he said apologetically as he slid a simple ring over her finger.

"I take this as a pledge of your love. That is the different I am looking for."

He stood up and kissed her. "Well then, congratulations Abigale Bates. This means you are now betrothed to an authentic fugitive from the law who is wanted for kidnapping."

"You know very well I was already captivated," she said with a smile.

"Likewise... Come. It is late, so we will stay at the camp. Let's savour the mountaintop tonight, for tomorrow we return to town to hide in plain sight.

❧❧❦❧❧

17

Abby spent a lot of time staring out the window. A woman chased a child around the corner with a switch. Old men smuggled cheap bottles of grog under their tattered coats to find an undisturbed corner to drink. Kids colluded in huddles, racking up mischief and pulling pranks on the unsuspecting. She could not get used to the unrelenting smell that constantly made her feel like heaving. She had no household to manage. She had no staff to supervise. The lack of useful occupation had her loathing the rooms at Greystone.

Ruben organised for Callie and Ted to share these upstairs rooms with Abby. It was a considerate arrangement, necessary for the safety and companionship of a lady. She applied a little scented lip-balm liberally to her top lip and picked up one of Ruben's books he had on his temporary office desk set up in the area that was the sitting area. The volume was a legal book, and the language was difficult with many strange terms. She read another page or two, and then put it down. She could only digest that literary fare in small servings, but she was getting through it.

She restlessly noticed that one of Ted's shirts was missing a button. She went to Callie's sewing kit and found a close match... and sewed the button on. It barely took her five minutes and then she stared out the window again. Eventually she went to the door and pinned on her hat. "Let's go for a walk Callie... perhaps down to the street venders. It is entirely appropriate that we have some constitutional walking. We need to keep you healthy until the baby comes."

Callie stared at her dubiously. She rubbed the growing profile of her belly and said nothing. She didn't move.

"Come, Callie don't be tardy. If you don't move along, I will go without you. This room is driving me to distraction!"

Within seconds Callie had her hat and shawl on. Abby grabbed her parasol, locked the door to their apartment and walked along the corridor. As they turned down the narrow stairwell, Ruben met them coming up. Her eyes lit up. He looked at her with a frown and Abby's face quickly sobered. "What is wrong? Do you not like this dress? It is newly made and a very fashionable choice. They said the blue in the check compliments my eyes."

He shrugged and turned her around and guided her back to their rooms. "Let's share a cup of coffee before I go back."

"Excellent idea," and she stoked the little wood stove and added the kettle.

Ruben nodded and quietly drew Callie aside, speaking with her earnestly. Abby looked at them locked in serious conversation while she waited for the water to boil. She took the kettle off and set his coffee to draw. "I fear that you are talking about me. What is the problem?"

"Oh Ma'am, it is a difficult situation that you are in," said Callie quickly.

Ruben pursed his lips thoughtfully. "You stand out like a glittering jewel in this quagmire of human filth."

"Aah... 'pearls-before-swine'; an age-old dilemma. Still, I didn't ask to live in squalor. I preferred the idea of being betrothed to a mountaineer."

"I have explained why we are here. It is close to the city and the library. It is a location that polite society avoids. So, it gives us access, and proximity, and complete invisibility. I do understand it is unpleasant."

Callie looked distressed. "I told Mr Ruben, Ma'am, that you are a lady. It is not your fault that you stand out."

Ruben's frown deepened. "If you go out, people will notice and our reach for invisibility will be compromised. It is unpleasant anyway, so I recommend you stay inside."

"That sounds distinctly like house arrest. I did not become engaged to stay under lock and key." Who ever thought that the mantlepiece would offer more freedom? She poured his coffee and set it on his desk.

He didn't look up as he rifled through some papers he had been working on the evening before. "No, but it is safer. It is not forever. I just came to collect a document. It will save me dropping in here on my way home this evening. I'll see you tomorrow." He added a couple of additional papers as an afterthought to his satchel, and then closed the door firmly as he left.

Abby stared after him bewildered. She picked up his untouched mug and took a mouthful of coffee before she tipped it out. He had spoken of his pursuit of a better world, but in a short space of time she was locked away in the useless cupboard where genteel women were kept. Was it an impossible ambition to be included and useful? Ruben was shutting her out of that glorious dream. His intention might be protection and care but shut-out or shut-in is still shut-away none the less.

She turned to Callie. "So, Callie, if the problem is that I stand out. Surely there is some way to have me blend in?"

Callie stared at her. It was evident she was reluctant to entertain the idea. "Ma'am... I could. But it ain't pretty to blend-in, and it would not be to your liking."

Abby shook her head. "You say that to test me. Do you think this is a challenge that I cannot rise to?"

"Mr Ruben may not be pleased. It would be very unpleasant."

"Callie, you are well aware that being locked up here is already unpleasant. So, if you have a way to disguise my boredom, then let's try it. It sounds like something I might be willing to attempt."

"Okay Ma'am... if you are determined. Choose for me your ugliest dress."

Abby smiled. "But I don't have ugly dresses. I gave them all away."

Callie grimaced. "You could choose one of mine?"

Abby looked at her, as Callie jiggled uncomfortably from one foot to another.

"Very well, I'll trade one of my dresses for one of your choice, from your wardrobe." Abby went to the closet where her dresses hung and pulled out one of the cotton dresses that Glady had made up for her. "After your baby is born, you could do with a new outfit."

"Oh Ma'am, not that one. It is my favourite on you."

"I know. Show me what I get for this."

Callie went into her room and came back out with a very worn, shabby ill-fitting dress. Ugly was not mistaken. She showed it to her embarrassed.

Abby looked at it dubiously. "Okay... And you want me to put it on?"

"Yes Ma'am. So, you can get the full effect."

Abby took a deep breath. "Great..." she said without any enthusiasm.

Callie retrieved Ted's bootblack and brushed down the hem. It looked like she had waded through a bog. Then she sewed patches to the skirt and bodice. Callie sat Abby down in front of the mirror. "Ma'am, normally you use makeup to make yourself look pretty. If you want to be invisible, you have to look poor and unhealthy. Rather than hide the dirt or bruises... we make it look like you have them. The women here cannot disguise them, even to go to the market."

Abby shook her head and smiled. "Can you not see the irony in this? Now that I have no bruises, I need to pretend I that I do?"

"It is what women live with here."

Abbey sighed. "Well, at least we have that in common. Go ahead Callie: make me invisible."

Callie covered the mirror with a shawl, then proceeded to apply blotchy patches of make-up with uneven strokes. She did up Abby's hair in a matted mess and even added some charcoal to her teeth. "Now Ma'am, please don't be upset with me... because this does not look like you at all."

"Well, I do understand this is the whole idea."

"You are completely hidden, Ma'am," said Callie quietly. She hesitated and couldn't bring herself to remove the shawl covering the mirror. "I am so sorry, Ma'am."

Abby impatiently pulled the cover aside. She gasped and sat staring at the person in the reflection. "Hmm. I think it needs one more thing." Abby went to the cupboard and pulled down a large hatbox and extracted an ungainly hat with large flowers on it. She tore some of them off and trampled the rim. And then added a garish sort of scarf. Finally, she was entirely satisfied with the result.

"Oh Ma'am... that is... not what I expected. Ma'am, I thought you would be embarrassed."

"Well one thing is certain, Callie – you are going to have to stop calling me 'Ma'am'."

"Oh... but what can I call you then, Ma'am?"

"Well, I'm thinking that since this is a disguise, a different name altogether is needed. This poor woman's name will be... Bee. From Abby... Ab-bee. Call me Bee." She went to a tin sitting on a shelf and pulled out a novelty hatpin with a large enamel bee on the end. She looked at it and smiled and pinned it on like a broach. This would be her signature mark: a humble bee, a weaver of honey... something sweet, with a bit of a sting. "Don't you think it is fitting that I also have a pseudonym? That is entirely in keeping with my association with outlaws and bushrangers. Let's test it out and see how we go? We shall buy something from the market for dinner."

Callie shook her head mystified, changed her dress, and gave herself a similar makeover. As they walked out onto the street, Callie offered a few more suggestions. "You walk too tall, Ma'am..."

"Bee."

"Very well: Miss Bee. Bee needs to slump some... and shuffle."

"Oh. Okay... like this?"

Callie smiled. "Yeah. I think that is better."

They stopped at a stall. Bee went to pick out a selection of potatoes, when Callie stepped forward, restraining her arm. "We want some potatoes," she said with a heavy accent.

Abby grimaced, and Callie quickly interjected. "Now Bee, don't be making a scene. I will tell them about the potatoes."

Abby pouted and again Callie spoke over her. "She's a bit stupid you know. Not quite all there upstairs like. But she's got a good kindly heart in her own way." The stall keeper sort of grunted and pushed the change to the few coins that Callie had scrounged from her pinafore pocket towards her. "She's my sister, but just 'cause she don't talk, don't mean she does any harm. Come Bee. Let's take the potatoes and go home." Bee gave a silly, dull sort of grin, and Callie took her by the hand and led her away.

❧❀❧

As they left and walked through a small alley, they passed a young mite of a girl sitting on an upturned box staring at the gutter running with filth. Abby gasped. Callie encouraged her to walk on, but Bee pulled her hand away, shuffled up beside her and sat down on another box. Bee said nothing, and the girl looked at her with eyes too large for her face. Bee picked up a stick and felt in her pocket and pulled out a small, tattered kerchief. She silently tore off a strip of rag and bound a cross piece of stick as arms. Then she poked the stick through the centre of the rag and wrapped it up tightly with a thread she pulled from its hem. She hummed a little tune and made the stick-doll dance. The girl's large eyes didn't move from the little performance. Bee danced the little doll over to the child and then left it in her lap. Then she stood up and silently took Callie's hand like a little girl and they walked away. As Bee silently stole a look over her shoulder, and saw the little girl seriously continue the dance with her new friend.

Bee was careful to say nothing until they were safety back in their rooms. She took off her hat and grubby pinafore and shuddered at the grime that was over her gloved hands as she peeled them off. "Excuse me, Callie but I need to wash." She went into her room and stood at the washstand, scrubbing her face and her hands. When she came out, she sat down in a clean dress and looked at Bee's costume sitting in a heap on the floor. "So? How effective was your potion? Did your enchantment make Bee sufficiently invisible?"

"Oh, Ma'am, you were amazing! I am so sorry about the story of you being a bit dull and stupid... but I thought it would be better if you don't talk... since you speak so elegant and nice."

"Well, that is the most fun I have had since coming to this neighbourhood. I have been so bored! But this has given me something to look forward to when Bee goes out tomorrow."

"Tomorrow, Ma'am? Oh. Do you think it is a good idea to do this too often?"

"I think it is entirely appropriate that I practice... and I want to see if that little girl is there again tomorrow."

Immediately, Abby got out her needle and thread and started sewing. She cut out fabric from a petticoat and a tablecloth. There was a peace in her industry that gave her great satisfaction. When Ruben came in the next morning, he nodded gratefully to see Abby doing something other than pacing.

She put down her project and came over to where he had settled at his desk working through some papers. "Are you making progress constructing your defence?"

He looked up and raised his brow, as if he didn't quite know how to answer her.

She looked at him severely. "Do you expect me not to be interested in such matters?"

"I... I do not want to worry you with matters that you cannot influence."

"Ruben Davey, don't show me another version of condescension. I have lived with it all my life, but I have never had it from you." Her eyes flashed with indignation and his jaw dropped.

"Surely being protective of my fiancé is not contempt of your capabilities?"

"I would say it is exactly that."

"How? This is messy and unjust and painful. You don't need it. I, however, have no choice in the matter. I must attend to it."

"Do you assume that I would not comprehend, or I might faint and not cope? Why should I not be interested in the issues that will see you either liberated or sent to the gallows?"

"Well, it is complicated...

"So, you think I am dull and stupid?"

"No, of course not. You have shown yourself to be intelligent in all sorts of matters."

"Then why do you exclude me?"

"I told you why. I would rather that you not be distressed by this."

"And so, you have decided that I don't get a choice? You didn't disturb yourself with protecting me from unpleasantness when you called me to assist with Jay's wound... or encouraged me to lead your corrupt possie of lawyers through the mountain-scrub."

"That was different. Now you are promised to be my wife."

"Conducting that tour into the hills, demonstrated that I am as committed as your men. If there is any difference, it is only that I am even more invested now that I wear your ring. I told you once, that given the choice, I am inclined towards useful service. Don't rob me of that option, Ruben. There is little I can do perhaps, but surely, I am allowed to support you through this! Who else do you have by your side through this unpleasantness?"

"I have told you that I will not expose you to unnecessary risk Abby. Even I underestimated their ruthlessness. These people will not hesitate to use you against me if they know we are to be married. That is a hand they cannot lose. You, Abby, are more valuable to me than my liberty, or reputation."

She softened and reached out and touched his face. "I know. But I miss the man who challenges me to dive deeper, and go further, and reach higher. I still treasure the idea that I can light a candle against the darkness that threatens you, and those around us."

"Oh Abby..." He pulled her into an embrace. "I... I am still learning how to be your intended. Forgive me. Perhaps I could find a way to be more open about the darkness we fight." He paused for a moment considering the challenge. "Well... what about... hmm, how would you feel about meeting Constable Wilson tomorrow? Rather than have you go out, I could bring him here as we discuss these matters."

She nodded eagerly. "What time?"

"I am meeting him for lunch."

"Then I will be ready for company," she said with a smile. And went back to work on her sewing project.

In the morning Abby quickly got Bee ready and this time she watched carefully as Callie applied her makeup. "We need to buy things for our lunch this afternoon," she said as they went to leave. Before they went out the door, Bee picked up her evening sewing projects. She tucked the simple rag doll in her pinafore pocket, as well as a handball she had made out of one of her stockings, stuffed and turned on itself, and stitched tightly in place. Abby checked her gait and adjusted her posture, took a deep breath, and gave a silly chuckle as she immersed herself in the disguise of Bee.

They walked to the market stalls, and Callie guided the simpleton Bee along the streets. She looked longingly at the little wooden boxes that stood empty in the alley. There was no sign of the little urchin who had danced with the dressed doll-stick. As they explored the market stalls, a scruffy kid sidled up behind them and Bee caught his arm with her good hand and held it firmly as he tried to extract some things from Callie's basket.

Abby thought quickly. "You my friend," she said with a lisp.

The kid looked at her queerly. "I ain't nobody's friend!" he said trying to release his hand.

"Then you must be my Callie's friend if you be takin' things from her basket," Bee insisted.

"I never did!" he vowed, wrinkling his freckled nose. "Never touched nothing!"

Not letting go of his wrist, she produced her sock handball. "Can you throw?"

He eyed the ball with anticipation. "Yeah. Better than you."

"Bet you can't," said Bee with a pout. She let him go as she tossed it in the air with her weak wrist and it fell awkwardly in a puddle. He picked it up and threw it back to her. She hadn't really expected him to throw it back and muddy water splattered all over her front as she caught it with a bit of a juggle.

He laughed. "See. I can throw good."

"Bet ya can't catch!" she said as she tossed it back to him.

He caught it with ease. "Hey Jimmy, gimme a go!" someone called, and soon a game was in full force as more kids joined them. Bee made it clear that the ball belonged to her friend Jimmy, and he stood tall from the status that it gave him.

In the middle of the game, she saw Ruben stop and talk to Callie. The ball hit her on the head with a bump. "Ow!" she cried rubbing her cheek.

Ruben stared at Callie's soiled dress with a frown. "Well, you know how to dress up to come to the market."

"Yes Sir. Just blending in. Mistress Abby wanted some things for lunch, since you are bringing a guest."

He glanced around. "I appreciate that you were able to convince her to stay indoors."

Callie almost corrected that assumption and then nodded. "She understands the importance of staying invisible, Sir," she said quietly.

"I'm surprised really. All the better that we understand each other. I'm on my way to meet her; did you need me to carry anything back for you?"

"No, Sir. Not many items really. Oh Sir, here is a key since Mistress is..."

"Resting? Well, I will see you shortly then. I won't disturb her as I have some reading to do," he said as he left. He smiled at the street-game of catch as the ball rolled to his feet. Bee quickly looked away. Ruben picked up the ball, tossed it back into the middle of the game, and went on his way down the street.

Just then Bee saw the little girl with the large eyes standing on the corner watching. She waved to her shyly and the girl waved back. The little girl's name was Mildred. Bee sat beside her as she clutched the little wooden stick wrapped in a rag. Bee pulled out the pocket rag doll and hummed the same song they shared yesterday. "Now you have two friends, Mildred," she said, as they danced her dolls together. Callie placed the items in her basket and Bee quickly ran back to her side to walk home.

While she wore Bee's clothes, Abby was entirely Bee. She wondered how Ruben would take her disguise. Callie stepped back as Bee came through the door carrying the basket.

Ruben glanced up from his book and frowned. "Callie! You can't invite people back here! I spoke about checking whether you are followed. I'm sorry Miss, you will have to leave."

"Leave?" she lisped.

"Shh! Please be quiet. Abby is asleep in the other room."

Abby sat down and proceeded to take off her frayed floral laden hat and scarf.

"Miss!" exclaimed Ruben in disgust.

Without a word, Callie brought over a basin of water and some cloths. Abby picked up the washer and began to wipe off her makeup.

Ruben stared at her in disbelief. "You cannot be in earnest?"

Abby offered a black-toothed smile and continued to wash her face. "That was quite some game of Catch-the-Ball," she said conversationally to Callie in her normal voice.

"Yes Ma'am, I think that your little Bee quite out did Jimmy and the boys on more than a couple of rounds. I think they will practice very hard so they best you next time." She passed Abby a hairbrush and they went into her room to help her take off her costume.

"That was *you* playing ball with those backstreet urchins?" gasped Ruben in horror through the door.

"Well, it was a friend of mine named Bee. I made that ball from one of my stockings." Abby slid off Bee's pinafore and dress and finished at the washstand in her petticoat. After she put on an apron over her tea-dress, she came through the door and smiled innocently at Ruben.

Callie's eyes went wide. "Ma'am! Your teeth!"

"Oh!" Abby quickly covered her mouth and went back to her room to remove the charcoal with the wooden-picks and brushes she normally used for cleaning her teeth. She gargled some water and then checked the mirror before she returned. "If you will excuse me, I believe we are expecting company for lunch." She watched Ruben sitting staring. The book before him stayed unread while she helped Callie prepare their meal. Callie had bundled up Bee's costume and folded it and put it aside out of the way, and Abby wordlessly put on the kettle to boil more water.

With the preparations for lunch complete, Abby again retreated to her room to freshen up, took off her apron and emerged elegantly prepared for company, with just a hint of lip colour, doused in a generous amount of lavender water and her hair simply arranged. Ruben still sat at his desk in a stunned sort of stupor.

As she passed by Ruben's desk she leant over and gently kissed his forehead. He grabbed her forearm. "You are still an independent, subversive, and rebellious woman," he murmured under his breath. "Abby, you need to be careful! I am serious."

She smiled benignly, unperturbed by his consternation. "One thing you will learn, Mr Davey, is that I have always been careful to comply with the wishes of the men in my life. My father had some very definite ideas about how my life could be to his advantage, which rarely included being up front and visible. At Mr Bates' insistence, I became very accomplished at being a perpetually benign neutral presence. And it seems you also require invisibility from me. In fact, I have become *so* proficient at obscurity that you demanded I leave my own home. This you cannot deny." She smiled and kissed the hand that held her arm.

"Yes, but..."

"But? Rather than being troubled by the humble Bee's ingenuity, think about how we can use it. There is potential here, I am sure. In the meantime, it gives me some industry that I have been craving." She looked at him and smiled faintly. "Welcome to *my* Meantime, Ruben Davey."

⁕⁂⁕

18

There was a rap at the door and Ruben answered it. Constable Harold Wilson quickly stepped inside, smoking restlessly. "You weren't followed?" Ruben checked. He shook his head and they spoke quietly while he removed his coat.

Abby smiled as she offered Harold a saucer to deposit his ash and the stub from his cigar. Abby was comfortable in her role as the gracious hostess, even in the face of all sorts of unsavoury male habits. She was grateful Ruben suggested this lunch meeting as a peace offering, showing he was willing to stand by his declaration to include her. They sat, said grace, and Abby laid out her expectation that at least during first course, social courtesies were to be attended to. She enquired after Harold's family, and found he was courting a young woman, who lived in the more pleasant parts of town. She was the daughter of a shop owner in the main town-centre and was herself a woman with a head for business. He blushed at Abby's enquiries and disclosed that he was saving for a ring and a deposit on a small apartment, as these matters were important to her father. He would not be a constable for long, as he was studying for his sergeant's stripes. There was room for progression in law-enforcement.

Ruben said nothing during this exchange and quietly ate his food. She quietly encouraged Harold to do what was needed to pursue his love. Abby stood to gather the plates, and on her return redirected the conversation to the purpose of their meeting as Callie poured tea and served cake. "Constable Wilson, how did you meet Mr Davey? Have you worked together before?"

"I made the arrests in the Inland Ambush case. It didn't seem likely that the charges would ever stick, but Davey put together a sound case. The public profile of that case has supported my ambitions to apply for advancement within the constabulary."

"So, would you agree that these latest allegations against Ruben are more vindictive than real?"

Wilson didn't miss Abby's transition from 'Mr Davey' to 'Ruben', but he sipped his tea without a flicker. He was sure there was more to his luncheon, then just an out-of-the-way venue. "I have no doubt Ma'am. But the evidence is scant. I will postpone any interrogations at the stationhouse for as long as I can. His willingness to be part of my investigation allows it."

"So, you believe Ruben can build a case to clear his name?"

"It is my wish... and my mission. I regard him well."

"Are you not concerned that this may injure your own reputation and desires for promotion?"

"We will continue to be discrete, until we have our case. I am confident that we can be of use to each other." He paused, waiting for Abby to leave so their discussion could proceed. She set her teacup down in its saucer and pushed aside her plate for Callie to remove, and then picked up her sewing. The constable restlessly stirred his tea and was obviously uncomfortable with her presence.

Ruben stirred. "Umm, I wanted Abby to stay. It is only right that she knows what is going on."

Harold's eyes widened slightly as if he suddenly registered something quite unexpected. "Oh! You are Mrs Abigail Bates!"

"I am."

"My apologies, Ma'am. We have never met. But... I understood you were abducted against your will."

She looked at him benignly and smiled, but when she spoke her voice was quietly firm. "Constable Wilson, do you take notice of the chatterings that would slander Ruben's name? Kidnapping is a serious accusation. Do you actually believe his innocence as you assert?"

"I thought... umm..." He seemed quite taken aback by her open challenge. "The witness accounts were consistent."

"There is a lot about my life that is not to my liking. Being close to Ruben is not one of them."

He turned to Ruben with a frown.

Ruben swallowed, paused, and then shrugged. "She was not abducted... but rescued. She was threatened by the very men who accuse me. I believe they were intent on murder, though it could never be proven. This hiding is necessary for her safety. She will be my wife; we are waiting for the six months of mourning to pass before we marry."

Wilson raised his brow and sipped his tea, his mind racing with this information. Ruben took up his pen and began to review various paths towards vindication, mapping out the detail on the pad. Wilson had little to add.

Abby continued to sew unobtrusively. Wilson's confidence grew, and he became more emphatic around where the sticking points of the investigation were. "There is still the problem of the misappropriated money. The trail on that money has gone stone cold. It has disappeared like an illusionist act! We need to find that money, and the perpetrator. That one step would automatically achieve all our goals of proving your innocence."

Ruben had been jotting notes over his charts. They had gone through a comparative list of potential suspects. "My name is still at the top of this list, but the position is circumstantial at best," he acknowledged with a frown.

Wilson reviewed the accusation of kidnapping of the Widow Bates. "Your disappearance has caused quite a sensation," he said with a swallow. "No disrespect intended, Ma'am," he qualified, and quickly added, "The incident has been leveraged to generate public outrage against Ruben. They have brought Rupert in to influence activating official resources."

Abby mildly rethreaded her needle. "It is not unexpected, Constable. We know their modus operandi," she said graciously, as she continued to stitch.

"But I fear your plan may have backfired. Now that I know you are here, I need to declare it." Ruben negotiated another fortnight of grace before he took that action. Abby raised her brow with a kindly smile and tied off a stitch. She extended her hand as she stood. "Well, it has been lovely meeting you Constable. This is a difficult time. I trust we can finally make some progress on this together."

Harold nodded as he picked his hat off the stand. "I am a public servant at your service," he said amiably as he put on his coat. "I am sure the conclusion of this matter will be quite satisfactory."

His assurance encouraged Ruben's waning confidence.

⁕⁕⁕

Bee went down to the market every day. While Callie did the shopping, she played ball with the boys and plied the girls with an assortment of stuffed rag toys that she had made, all embroidered with the signature motif of a little bee. But it was the bread buns that they bought, which opened up their hearts. They invited her into their world through games of hide-and-seek, hopscotch, and tag. Jimmy had the best haunts that he showed her. She learnt their neighbourhood and their ways from the inside. This was a way to light a candle against their appalling situation. At the end of the day, she had the relief of going home and Callie would draw her a bath. That was the tragedy of it all. She didn't have to stay there, and they did.

19

Abby jolted awake. Ted was with Ruben, meeting the men in the caverns along the range. Did this mean their business was concluded early? She lay very still. Muffled cries from the next room set her heart beating loudly in her throat. She reached out to locate the heavy base of her reading lamp in the dark, and she pulled it over to her. Her wrist ached from the weight, but she clung on tight as she quickly slid out from under the covers. That familiar, stifling fear that would send her hiding from Sorenson choked her. She opened the door to the closet and pushed back behind the skirts and petticoats, clutching the cold lamp-base to her chest, oil trickling down her nightdress. She saw the wavering flicker of a torch through the crack in the door and heard their rough expletives as they discovered her vanishing act and rummaged the room in search. She tried to stay perfectly still, but her wrist started trembling uncontrollably, aching in its weakness. She clutched the lamp hard against her chest with other her hand and immobilized its unsteadiness. Suddenly a hatbox tumbled from the top of the wardrobe, crashing loudly to the floor. There was a pause, and then the door of the robe was thrown open. The torchlight shone in her face. She launched the lamp-base at the light, and it hit her target solidly. It burst into an explosion of light as the oil ignited. He cursed loudly, and dropped the torch in his hand, grabbing at a rug on the bed to smother the flames. Abby lashed out, but he dragged her by her hair to the middle of the room. Another frame loomed in the shadows behind the bright flare of his torch. Bandanas concealed their features distorting the shadowy shapes in the surreal dance of orange light. The muffled cries of Callie penetrated her fear and she made herself go limp. Submission was her protection; she didn't dare struggle.

Two men dragged Callie to the door. "Stop!" Callie groaned.

They roughly pushed Abby into the main room. "You can see she is pregnant. Please, don't hurt her!"

"Then shut up!"

She nodded mutely and grabbed their coats from the rack by the door. The stand crashed to the floor, as they stumbled down the stairs. Abby's mind spun with a kaleidoscope of images: flames, light, shadow, ropes, horses, cart, dark. These men were coarse and certain, experienced highwaymen. That she would actually be abducted, when those charges were sticking like wet mud to Ruben's reputation, smacked her in the chest like an ironic cruel fist.

Abby gave up trying to work out where she was. The cart was rough and smelly, stifling under a cover of heavy oilcloth. The ties on her wrists and ankles were tight, and with every jolt they dug in sharply as they lurched over potholes and ruts. She could feel Callie beside her in the dark, groaning. The fear was suffocating; she dreaded this relentless jarring on her friend's heavily pregnant body. The wagon stopped and the voices spoke in a muffled volley. Nothing was clear. Then there was another voice, just as crass and rough, but with an edge that made her skin go cold.

Somewhere, the noises of town merged into the quiet of the bush, and it silence seemed to amplify the panic in her chest. After an eternity the cart heaved to a stop; the canvas cover was ripped back. They were dragged off the tailgate and the ropes on their ankles cut. Abby stumbled and he roughly yanked her upright. Forward. She was pushed through a doorway, and she fell to the floor. She could hear Callie stumble in beside her and a heavy door slid into place, rattling closed behind them.

Abby lay still for a time, listening. Silence. Except for whimpering there was little she could discern. She edged closer in the dark, to offer comfort. But then she heard Callie speak up from the other side. "Ma'am? Ma'am!" she whispered.

Abby quietly whispered a response.

"My hands are bound strong. Are yours tight? I thought I might be able to loosen the bands. Where are you? Keep talking... yes... I am coming."

They found each other in the dark. Abby raised her wrists and Callie manoeuvred the rope with her teeth. Slowly but surely the knot loosened. She wriggled her wrists free and worked the rope on Callie wrists slowly, until it came free.

Abby rubbed her aching wrists. "Are you okay? Are you hurt? The baby?"

"I feel like I been rung through a mangle Ma'am. The little one is moving still so I think we are fine."

"Oh Callie. I have been so worried."

"He is tough, Ma'am. Tough like his dad."

Abby sighed with relief in the dark. "And his mother."

The smell of hay and straw clinging to their clothes denoted they had been dumped in some sort of hay-shed. They edged closer to the muffled cries in the dark. Their eyes adjusted to the blackness, and they felt the other prisoner flinch at their touch. "Shh... Ma'am. We were able to loosen our ties. If we unbind your gag, please will you promise not to scream? It would be better if they didn't know we are not bound."

The muffled groans increased hysterically. As they leaned forward, they could see the whites of her eyes bright with terror and her dishevelled hair gave her a maniacal look in the deep shadows. Abby spoke to her again, gently, calmly. "Just breathe. Breathe... Breathe... We must be quiet. So quiet." Her muffled cried intensified. And Abby stepped away. "Callie, I can't risk her screaming if we remove the gag. They will come back. I don't want them realising we are not tied." They groped back around in the dark and found their discarded ties. They played with the ropes around their wrists, so they could replace them quickly in a way that might be convincing, if they were not examined too closely.

Abby went back to their companion. "Shh. Promise that if I remove your bindings, you will be quiet?"

The woman nodded frantically. Abby gently loosened the gag and she gasped for air as one who had been drowning. Callie soothingly stroked her arm, and the woman clung to her like a life raft.

"Ma'am... what is your name?" Abby asked gently after a while.

"Fra... Francine M... Moore," she gasped.

"Mrs Moore?" Abby looked hard at her wild hair and dust-smeared makeup... and she thought of Bee's disguise.

"Yes! Yes! Mr Moore will see justice served! This delinquency we are subject to is a travesty beyond reason!" Her voice started to sound shrill.

Abby frowned and held her finger to her lips. "Shh. Mrs Moore... it is Abby Bates. You have shared tea with me at Redwood Park. I know this is hard, but we must stay contained." She shook her head, confused, and pictured the cold Mr Moore, reneging on his signature in Ruben's cavern. "Your husband... I'm sure he is doing all that he can."

Francine tilted her head higher. "Yes! Yes! Of course! It is blatantly shameful that I should be treated so."

"Oh yes, Ma'am, on this we all agree."

They sat waiting to see if those guarding their compound would show themselves again, but even after the long hours of night there was still no movement outside. A dingo howled and the call of a boobook owl echoed around the dark. The waiting became oppressive. Mrs Moore offered a whispered commentary on the dreadfulness of her abduction; the virtues of her husband; the diversion of her society; the amusing antics of her lapdog Dewy; the tastefulness of her wardrobe; the health of her diet; the detail of her toilet; the merits of her privileged society. By the time the first streaks of dawn finally filtered through the timber slab walls where they were held, they knew it all.

Abby took a look around, absorbing all the details of the hayshed. There were aged signs of previous occupation, of the human and the sheep kind. She stood and looked between the slats on the large heavy doors. There was no movement outside to suggest any of their abductors had stayed to guard them. Perhaps they had been dumped and abandoned like stray cats. She could see no other buildings, just miles and miles of grass merging into scrub.

She rattled the door. The chain secured from the outside, clanged harshly. Firmly locked. There were no other doors. No windows. She went around the walls checking all the timber slabs, to see if any were loose or rotting. For a primitive structure made from scrub timbers, it was built like a stone fort. Their gaoler had left a box and a bucket of water near the door. There was another empty bucket that she supposed was to be used as a toilet. There was some damper inside the box and a slab of salted mutton. They shared it among themselves for breakfast, then Abby laid back against the hay, trying to think.

Mrs Moore, as the wife of the partner in the Firm *Crosby and Moore* may be worth money, but who would demand a ransom for a disenfranchised widow and a domestic servant? That made no sense. Only trusted friends knew of her connection with Ruben, but somehow, the address of their invisible residence in the slums had leaked out. She looked up into the rafters willing some clarity to fall from the sky. Maybe they could dig under the slatted walls. Or a loose shingle may be their way out. Dig dirt that was compacted like concrete, without implements? Climb rafters with a fully pregnant mother? And then what? She had no idea where they were!

⁕⁂⁕

They dozed in the warmth of the day. Mrs Moore continued to rage over the injustice of their position, and the slits of light faded through the slats again to conclude their day. Abby marked a calendar into the wall. She knew how disorientated they could become. One night, one day passed. It had already seemed like a week. Sometime during the next night, they heard a cart drive up. The horses were restless, and the driver had the same sound about him. The door groaned as it was opened, and the man pushed another person through to the floor. He lifted the lantern and looked at them cowering quietly, the ropes on their wrists all in place. The lamp-light clearly illuminated his face. Abby gasped and turned away. He dumped a hessian bag into the box and sloshed another bucket of water beside it. The inhumanity sent Abby's blood boiling. She regretted not setting an ambush, but three women: one hysterical, one pregnant and herself uncertain, against an armed captor didn't seem to carry much authority.

131

When the cart left, they shed their binds and went over to the woman clumped in a heap near the door. They lifted her up. She groaned, and they released her binds. "Oh Ma'am. Where did they hurt you?" asked Callie gently as they massaged her wrists where the ties had left marks.

"My head thumps. I was knocked out I think."

"Come and lie down. I'm sorry we can only offer a little water and some bread. Here you are – but there is hay at least to lie on."

She groaned again and rolled onto her side holding her head. "Where are we?"

"We are not sure. My name is Abby. This is Callie, and Mrs Francine Moore."

"Francine? It's Caroline. Caroline Winnicott. What is going on?"

"Caroline Winnicott? Oh, my goodness Caroline this is outrageous!" Francine burst into tears. Callie made an attempt to soothe her, but Francine refused to be consoled.

Abby frowned into the dark. What sort of audacious scheme was going on here? Caroline Winnicott? Now this lady was *really* worth money. Lots of money. More than Moore. It seemed beyond reason.

Where was the common connection? Her mind struggled to formulate a diagram like on Ruben's note pads. Eventually Abby had to concede there was a consistent denominator: she was. Callie was her attendant. Sorenson had been a client of Mrs Moore's husband, and Francine was part of that fashionable circle her life at Redwood Park demanded. The Moore's and Winnicott's were established recipients of the reserved seating at the Shearer's Feast. Although Abby had been a mainstay Winnicott customer, she had not reviewed their fabric collections since the funeral. This seemed to be more about her past life than her current one. Was this her punishment for turning her back on society in her widowhood? The belief that she was getting her life back seemed more whimsical than the actual reality. Ruben's fearful claim that they would use her to come after him, didn't seem the likely motivation... not with Mrs Moore sitting in the straw beside her. Abby couldn't sleep, trying to follow the tattered threads of association; tracking the twisted lines hoping that some clearer pattern would emerge; praying that in some way Ruben would be back sooner than anticipated from their gathering in the hills, and he would be able to find where they were. She prayed, desperately holding on to the hope of her freedom, Ruben's vindication, and that the conclusion to this nightmare was not out of reach.

⁂

20.

Ruben came along the path and stepped over the gutter. He looked up doubtfully at the little rented rooms and noticed with a frown that no light shone in the window. He loosened a brick and extracted the spare key. He walked up the stairs cautiously. The lock was broken and the door ajar. He pushed it back slowly. He stood for a moment and then lit the lamp on his desk. He stared around at the chaos as he lifted the lamp higher. He stepped into the bedroom and saw the scorched quilt on the floor, the open closet, the smashed bed lamp on the floor, the crushed hat-box. It told a tale.

He checked the drawer where he knew where Abby kept her few remaining pieces of jewellery and the money her pawned offerings had made. The little locked box was still there at the back of the drawer. He pushed it in and, and then on second thoughts, put the box in the space behind the drawers, and turned thoughtfully back to the living room. He scanned through the piles of papers on his desk. It seemed that none of his notes were missing, or even disturbed. There was no sign of a ransom note. The mantle clock was stopped. He frowned. He knew that to be a Sunday ritual. That was three days ago. His fiancé and her attendant had disappeared. No theft. All his records on his investigation were where he had left them. To do this, they had to have known he and Ted were away. Their invisible refuge was exposed. He blew out the lamp, closed the door and went straight to Dickens' place.

There was a pause before Dickens answered his knock, with a candle in his hand. "Where's Ted?" Ruben asked without ceremony.

"He went home to his Missus."

"I just came from there. They are both gone."

"Blue and his girl?"

"No Callie and Abby. They're gone. Ted wasn't there."

Dickens swore and moved back from the doorway as Ruben walked inside and sat down.

"Wasn't a robbery. Just a mess. Looks like they put up a fight," said Ruben, running his hand through his hair.

"Huh. They'll be here soon enough then. You know how they've been," said Dickens.

"I thought we sorted it. I'm as frustrated as the rest." He briefly considered what Dickens alluded to: that discontent would cause his men to erupt. Who could really be trusted? Without exception, his men had solid alibis this past week: himself and each other. "Abby was discovered, and they have come after me." How could he protect her when she refused to listen and lay low? He felt sick to his stomach.

There was a rap at the door. Jay was there. "Got a message for Dickens from Cook. She said Ruben's mate from the Law firm... that Big Wig... Moore... well, his wife has gone missing: a couple of days ago."

"Missing?" said Dickens staring at Ruben.

Ruben stared at them both and shook his in disbelief. "Herbert Moore's wife?"

He shrugged. "Guess so. The name was definitely Moore: Crosby and *Moore*. That was where you used to work, hey?"

He nodded. "His wife is the most fragile, untempered creature. She will not cope."

"Boss? This ain't no coincidence: both gone together so close. Do you reckon this is part of the one and same matter? Why would the firm use Mistress Abby and Callie as leverage to get to you and then abduct one of their own?" Dickens' question hung in the air like the putrid smell of refuse clouding the atmosphere.

"Then it must come from some other quarter. Wilson has got to have some idea on what's going on. I'll go back to the flat and see if I can find some trace of how this fits together." He reached for his hat. But as he opened the door, Ted was there with the other men. They pushed Ruben back inside, swearing out threats against him.

Dickens squared his shoulders and stepped in front of Ruben. "Steady on fellas. This is not the Captain's doin'."

"They've got Callie!" screamed Ted, his face as red as his hair. "Don't be telling me it not his doin', because I ain't seeing it that way."

"Blue! They have Abby too!"

Another stepped forward. "Maybe so, but he's not doing much to fix it!"

"They'll come after all our kin next!" another bellowed.

They flexed their fists and their tempers, pushing forward. Their eyes fully intent on avenging their fear. Dickens and Hawk stepped between them, shoulder to shoulder: a wall of bulk and muscle, not shy of bad manners if required. That was the remedy needed, and the stand-off was short. Gradually they stood down.

Ruben stood on a chair. "Men! You need to go to your families to make sure they are safe: don't delay! You are absolutely right. Our loved ones are our priority. There is no point fighting to make for a better community if our very homes are left exposed behind us. And right now, we are very exposed. In taking Callie and Abby they have taken something from all of us! Each one of our homes are violated by implication. They want us to believe we are no longer safe! That every family is no longer secure!"

The ripple of muttering ran through the group. Ruben watched a number storm away. Some wanted to find out what was behind it all. Ruben cleared his throat, rasped by the anger burning there. "Men, if you feel you can add manpower to this search, I appreciate your willingness. But we do this together. We don't turn on each other. We are brothers, not the enemy. We stand opposed to those who have dared this reckless act against those we love."

A couple declared the impossibility of boxing ghouls and phantoms; they left as well. Ruben looked at those who remained and nodded his appreciation. A gallant few. "Hawk, can you call on your cousin? We'll need his experience tracking. When they said we are pursuing ghosts, they are not far from the mark. We can't do much until sun-up; catch a kip while I find Wilson. Anything he's discovered will hopefully give us somewhere to start at first light."

⁂

Ruben scanned the alley as he walked along, keeping to the shadows. The slums were still, excepting the occasional yelp or a smashing glass accompanied by a drunken volley of swearing. Nothing seemed different here. He stepped over the puddles, his mind racing. How could he ever secure his own defence when there was always another urgent fire that needed putting out? He pulled his overcoat around him and moved in closer to the shadows, looking at the moon spill through a break in the clouds. It shone onto the dark muddy ground offering streaks of light in the murky puddles lying in the ruts on the street.

Was this divine retribution because he had fallen in love with a woman who was already married? Those feelings were unwitting and unintended, but he had been so strict about keeping his manner proper.

137

He never touched her. He never spoke tenderly to her. Ruben had been so mindful that she was untouchable, yet their hearts connected. Was it arrogance to assume that his private torture had been his vindication? Now that she was in great danger, he was sure the penalty of his sins had fallen on her innocence.

He was shaken by how quickly his men had turned against him. And he wondered if Abby would be as shocked as he was by their mutiny. Didn't she try to warn him of this? Why should their anger wound when he had insisted that he was merely a conductor at a way-station to the next thing? Perhaps they felt abandoned by the confession that he was waiting too, marking time to get out. Perhaps he had laboured the idea of *Meantime* too much. He intended to offer the notion as encouragement – just as it had for him: that this too will pass. That regardless how hard circumstances are now, there is always more down the line that God has in store.

When he had proposed taking the men away... to sort these matters through... allowing them to voice their concerns and fears, they seemed on board. The time they had spent back in the caverns of Gilyard Range had strengthened their purpose, and their resolve to see this through. He had logically showed how he was here for them. He had stayed! He was available! But then, as soon as the weather turned grey, he realised they hadn't heard him at all.

He heard steps following and leaned against a recess in the cold brick wall in the dark. The steps paused with him. His muscles coiled, like a sprung trap ready to snap. He scanned his life in a sort of out-of-body awareness. He was grateful at least that God would hear him because he had few others whose counsel could he really lean on. Dickens was sure, as was Hawk. And Wilson. His support had been unwavering since the Ambush Case. And then there was Abby. He regretted his insistence on keeping her at arm's length. Was it really protectiveness, as he had so confidently asserted? Or fear... dread that such transparency would expose that the smart lawyer didn't have any answers after all? How he wished right now, he could go and wake Abby up and hold her in his uncertainty and disclose his strangling fear and infuriating anger that was threatening to rupture any moment.

He moved on again, and sure enough, the steps followed, so he backed into another dark alcove. Still and silent, he took a deep breath. "God, our Father which art in Heaven, hallowed be thy name..." Then he abandoned the formality of the familiar prayer, and tumbled his thoughts, uncensored and unfiltered, into the hand of God. He prayed his terror, his anger, his confusion, his rejection... and willed his God to infuse wisdom where he honestly didn't have a clue. He prayed until he felt trust leak through the hard wall of his fear. He nodded. Yes, the Divine could sift through his confusion and offer some direction and protection. He took a deep breath in. Yes. He didn't know how or where or why. But God did. And that offered him a measure of courage and strength. Courage that was not fear-*less* but moving forward through the horror of it all.

Ruben jolted from his thoughts as he heard another footfall, barely distinguishable, instinctively he coiled and then pounced as he calculated the progress of his tracker. He hurled him up against the wall grasping at the grip of his handgun that had been concealed under his coat. In the weak streaks of moonlight, he peered into the eyes of a small frame. "You're a kid? What are you doing following me out in the middle of the night?"

"Mister, are you Miss Bee's friend? Me think she in trouble, Sir."

He released him and brushed his tattered coat, as he stood him to his feet. "Do you know where she is?"

"Nup. Haven't seen her. And that's the problem. She always came. Bought us bread. It's strange. She hasn't been around for a couple of days now. Her place is dark and still. That ain't right either."

"What's your name, son?"

"Are you her friend? I ain't inclined to talk if you're a Coppa. Seen you with that Wilson bloke."

"I'm not police. My name is Ruben. Ruben Davey."

"Oh. You're that guy. Well, that should be okay then... since the Coppas are looking for you."

"They are?"

"Been askin' about. Rumours they heard you'd moved in around here."

"Oh."

"I'm Jimmy. Bee's friend."

"Jimmy. Yes, Ab...Miss Bee has mentioned you. Well, a friend of Bee's is a friend of mine."

"Me thinking I know who took her... more or less."

"You do?"

"Yeah. But I don't know where to."

"Who?"

"Pittman. Got a scar on his cheek. Mean as a cut snake."

"Why do you think it's him?"

"He takes those sorts of jobs. They gave him money; then the next couple of days – she's gone. That's gotta mean something. Here it does anyways."

"Someone paid for her to be abducted?"

"Sure... Pittman don't do nothing for free."

Ruben eyes flew wide as the conspiracy expanded. "Do you know who would pay him?"

"Of course. Anyone who wants to keep their respect-able nose clean. The scar guy – Pittman, well he ain't respect-able. He'll do anybody's dirty work, and not too fussy about the price. Lots of respect-able people use him for that."

"Can you show me where to find this Pittman?"

"Sure. But I ain't doing it for you. I'm doing it for Bee. I ain't free either."

Ruben rummaged in his pocket for a coin. "Sure. I'd be doing it for Bee as well." He went to follow him. "Jimmy. When was the last time you ate?"

"Dunno. Day before yesterday... maybe."

"Hmm. How about we go back to Bee's place? I'll fix you a feed while we make a plan."

They walked back along the street to the rented rooms and climbed up the stairs. Ruben paused. He had closed the door, but it now stood ajar, the lock still dangling awkwardly. He signalled to Jimmy to be still, and he pulled out his handgun, walking quietly through the door. He carefully checked the rooms. They were deserted, and he drew the curtains closed before he lit the lamp and turned it down low. This time, every corner of the room was completely tossed.

Ruben went to the pantry and offered Jimmy a sandwich. The bread was stale and hard. "Bee's bread is usually better than this," he said, but he ate it hungrily. He took a drink and looked around. "I reckon whoever done this don't like you much, hey?"

Ruben went over to the desk and started to restack the scattered papers. The notations on his case were missing. Ruben rebuked his own stupidity. How could he leave his notes unprotected when he knew their position had been compromised!

"Don't you know where you are? This is Greystone," Jimmy said with shrug as he spoke around a mouth-full of sandwich. He considered Ruben ridiculously naïve... perhaps even more stupid than his friend Bee. But Bee was a good sort, even if her upstairs had an alley-cat or two running loose. Jimmy scoffed the rest of his sandwich, made another and stuffed that one down his britches. "If we go now, I can show you where Pittman hangs out. We could tail him to where they got her."

Ruben followed Jimmy through the streets. They crept around the back lanes, through broken palings, skirting known areas of surveillance, as the morning pre-dawn sounds began to stir. A dog howled. Sparrows started their chirping. A rooster crowed. A cat yowled as a mutt scrapped and chased it under a fence. Jimmy crouched behind some old wooden packing boxes that were rotting in the weather beside an equally dilapidated fence. He pointed. "That's his missus." A dark haired, thick set woman emerged from the back door and tipped her night-waste out into a gutter that ran along her side boundary. There was a volley of cusses as Pittman emerged. His bandana tied around his neck; a hat jammed down low over his ears. He picked up a hessian bag and walked quickly out along the street towards the community livery yard. Jimmy gestured Ruben to follow. "He looks like he's nothing, but he does okay. He's got a horse." That was the pinnacle of success in Jimmy's experience. Pittman strapped the hessian roll to the back of his saddle and rode out.

Ruben quickly hired a horse from the stable-hand. It was a skittish sort of mount, but when he hoisted Jimmy up in front of him, the kid was grinning ear to ear. "He went that way," said Jimmy pointing to the road out of town. "Not the first time he done this, but I could never follow him far."

"Let's see if we can today then. Hang on..." and he rode out, the sound of hooves thudding on the dirt road, echoing in the morning stillness.

❧❧❧❧❧

21

Ruben didn't consider himself a tracker, not in the manner of Hawk's cousin. But the clear route, the fresh rain, and the low morning traffic made his trail pretty obvious. The turn-offs had clear fresh hooves imprinted on the damp edges of the track. They were heading out into the valley. Why would they take Abby back to her family haunt? Did they expect her to stay the grieving widow forever? Was this about her abandoning the Bates' empire? Had Rupert taken over his father's possessive abuses? He doubted that. Someone as savvy as Rupert Bates would keep their distance, especially if he had been the money behind the contract. No, she would not be at Redwood Park. He felt a surge of confidence. This was familiar territory. Pittman's witlessness gave an advantage he might have otherwise not have had.

Ruben scanned his mind for likely out-of-the-way-places that could be used. He quickly narrowed it down to three possibilities: the caves in the hills; the hermit's shacks on the boarder-lands of Yellow Creek Station; or the barn out the back of Shipman Downs. The inconvenience of navigating the inaccessible range made that an unlikely choice. The hermit had a reckless reputation, and his broken-down, burnt-out hovels would hardly be secure enough for a reliable prison. That left the shed as the most likely possibility. It had been connected to a shepherd's hut at one point. The hut burnt down, and the shed became obsolete, except for storing excess hay from good seasons. It was secure, isolated: the perfect holding cage.

Ruben secured the horse in the shade along the creek and skirted the main track to the shed. Jimmy followed closely like a shadow. The door was old, but the chain and padlock were new. Pittman emerged carrying a bucket of water from the creek. Jimmy sneaked around the back of the shed. Inside he could hear groans: muffled and agonising.

"Bee! Bee!" he whispered fiercely through the cracks in the slab walls.

"Hello? Who is it? Please help us!" came the urgent plea.

"Bee! It's me! Jimmy…"

"Jimmy! How on earth did you find us? We need help! You have to go and get help!"

"Mister Ruben is here. He's come for you."

"Oh, Jimmy, please hurry!" she whispered urgently.

Pittman took the bag from his saddle. As he struggled with the key and padlock, Ruben stepped up with his gun drawn. "Slowly now, open the door," Ruben said firmly.

Pittman jolted and raised his rough brow, assessing his situation. He shrugged and raised his hands.

"Open the door," Ruben repeated.

He rattled the padlock and then as the chain ran lose Pittman grabbed the end, pulled it free, flung it around whipping it across Ruben's face. His handgun spun out of his hand, he screamed, holding his brow as blood poured, buckled in pain. Pittman slogged him across the jaw before he could regain his footing, and quickly had him pinned to the ground. "I know who you are," Pittman muttered through his stained, leering teeth. "Smart lawyers, aren't so smart,"

Jimmy dived deep into his pockets and pulled out his handball. He pelted it hard at Pittman face and hit him smack across the bridge of his nose. His head lurched back, and his nose started to bleed. In the pause Ruben struggled up as Jimmy skedaddled in and retrieved the gun, waving it recklessly, demanding Pittman stand up and away.

Pittman leered at Jimmy. "You don't know what to do with that. That ain't a toy Kid. Why would they send a kid to do a man's job.?"

Jimmy waved it wildly. His finger hit the trigger and a bullet ricocheted off the barn wall. "Move away I tell you!" he screamed.

Pittman's eyes narrowed. "Hey. I know you. You are Vera's ratty little sprite. Her good-for-nothing nephew. You don't have what this takes kid." Ruben blinked hard as blood trickled into his eyes, and shook his head as pulled himself up off the ground, welts roughly swelling around the gashes across his face. He grabbed the chain on the ground beside him and spun it fast, the links whipping around Pittman's legs in a rush. Ruben yanked the chain; the bucket of water beside the door sloshed over and Pittman fell hard, sprawling in a watery wave of mud. Ruben held him down, bound his hands with the rope from the saddlebag. He stood up unsteadily and took the gun from Jimmy's shaking hand. "You might be a kid, but this particular kid has taken down a criminal. I think Pittman here failed to recognise that, hey Jimmy? Quite the law-enforcer," he said proudly as he shook his hand.

Jimmy grabbed Ruben's shirt and pulled him towards the shed door. "Bee's in here. She's hurt."

Ruben tuned in to the muffled groans from inside. He pulled opened the door wide, light streaming into the shadows. Callie was on the floor pillowed by lumps of straw; sweat beading on her brow, tears streaming down her face. She looked up and saw Ruben and let out an unholy scream, and then started panting breathlessly. Abby knelt beside her. The bucket inside was all but empty and she offered Callie another sip from an old can. Two other women, one of them Moore's wife, crouched out of the way.

Ruben looked directly at Abby's ashen face. "She's in labour?" he said with a frown.

Abby nodded, then she grabbed the bucket and was sick. "We need a midwife."

"We are not far from Redwood Park. We could take her to the homestead. Get a message to Ted."

"Is this where we are? Oh...of course, the old Shepherds' barn on Shipman's place. I've heard of it, but never actually..."

Callie groaned and then screamed as another contraction gripped her.

"How far apart are they?" asked Ruben.

"I don't know. I have no..."

Miss Winnicott spoke up. She held a fob watch in her hand. "Two minutes apart. They have been like that for half an hour, or so."

"Oh." Abby looked dazed. She had almost forgotten the other women were huddled there in the shadows.

"Abby. Can I speak... privately?"

She nodded mutely and stood up wringing her hands, her nightgown smeared with grime. Ruben drew her aside. "Abby. Look at me. You can do this. You have to!"

"Ruben I am not a midwife! I have never had children. I have never even seen an alley cat have kittens. I have no transferrable knowledge here. Callie needs proper help."

"Yes, she does," he said in a measured tone. "And you are here. If she is that far along, we can't move her. A saddle horse is not an option now. I'll ride over and alert Gillis. He will dispatch for the midwife... doctor ... send a cart, and..." He looked at her with his serious eyes. "You are in illustrious company Abby. Take heart. Giving birth in a stable made quite a splash once."

"Oh, Ruben, that is not funny. Not Callie. She is my closest friend. What if it goes wrong? It can you know. Sometimes it does go wrong!" She almost hissed at him in her fear.

"I know. Ted and Callie are my friends too." He paused then, almost as if he had never really considered the truth of that assertion. "We will pray for a safe delivery: for both of them. Our responsibility lies in doing everything we reasonably can. Are you with me?"

Echoes of the caverns in the hills whispered a message of comfort. She nodded, and then jolted as Callie screamed again and she quickly returned to her side.

Ruben straightened up and squared his shoulders. Another spot fire was flaring up that could potentially get away, blowing out of control into a raging bushfire. "Now. There are practical things we can do. Ladies. I am going down to get some fresh water in the buckets. While I am gone, I need to you take off your petticoats."

"Mr Davey!" Mrs Moore blushed bright red.

"Mrs Moore, I mean no disrespect. We don't have linen or towels, but we can use your layers. If you are willing to share their abundance for the care of Callie's bairn, it would be appreciated. Move the soiled hay away and bring some fresh straw over here. We have a baby on its way. Abby? Logically birthing is a natural thing: help Callie work with this. You can do that. Jimmy! You're with me."

Pittman spat at them as they passed, and Jimmy had to run to keep up with Ruben's long legs on the way to the creek. "Hey Mister, why is Bee talking like that? And how come she is pretty now? She hardly seems like the same person."

Ruben almost grinned. He had thought her messed hair and soiled attire had all the dishevelled look of her disguise. "Well Jimmy, it is not usual for ladies to wear night gowns in public, but that's what she had on when they took her. She certainly is the same kind soul as before... just different externals."

Jimmy looked at him strangely. Weird. They washed the sick out of the bucket and then filled both of them with fresh water. As Ruben stepped back into the shed, a new sense of order formed. He put down the buckets, picked up the discarded ropes and went and secured Pittman's ties even further, before he mounted up and rode over to the Redwood Park Station, cutting a direct route across the creek and paddocks.

Abby sat with Callie, supporting her through each contraction. She reminded her of the times Callie had helped the wives of farm-hands and the maids. And Abby found that breathing through each contraction with her, helped settle her own strangling fear. It was forever before they heard Ruben ride back in.

As the next contraction eased, Abby stood up and went out to Ruben. He and Jimmy were gathering brush, and wood. "What are you doing?" she asked.

He shrugged. "I brought back a billy and a flint to make a fire, so we can heat some water. Help is on its way."

"Under different circumstances we would have a midwife and attendants swarming over her. But we don't. You cannot sit out here by the fire and have no part in this."

"Lighting a fire is a useful occupation while you attend to Callie. You know I can't go in there. Mrs Moore would be scandalised."

Another scream split the air.

"Mrs Moore has suffered so much that scandal is no longer the primary offence."

"You want me inside? While a woman is giving birth? Mrs Bates, your sense of the appropriate is getting quite loose. Your friend needs *you*... not me."

"Yes! Unusual it is. But you would do no less for your horse if it was in foal. And Callie is more precious to me than any animal. I need you with me. Caroline Winnicott has her hands full with Mrs Moore."

"Winnicott? The other woman is Winnicott's daughter?"

"Yes. Please, Ruben. You say I can do this... perhaps you are right: in this matter I have no choice. But I won't be doing it alone. I need you Ruben... do this, at least for Ted and Callie and their unborn baby!"

He saw the anxiety firing in her eyes. It reminded him that courage was not immunity to fear but doing what needed to be done despite it. Abby was one courageous soul. "If Callie allows it..."

Abby quickly took Callie's shrug as permission and gestured urgently for him to come inside. He stood behind Abby, his eyes averted, his hand on Abby's shoulder as she spoke reassuringly to Callie through her contractions. She felt his strength infusing her. Time ticked, and Abby started to shake. Ruben portioned out the bread among the ladies in the corner and made Abby take a bite. He offered them all a drink. He put both hands on her shoulders and she felt his presence stabilising her as he whispered reminders to breathe slowly, confidently, surely. She continued to tend her friend, offering her sips, wiping her brow with a piece of petticoat that had been torn from the offerings from the ladies in the corner.

Time seemed to move slowly, punctuated only by regular panting and the cries through contractions. Suddenly Callie started pushing with spontaneous intensity. Screaming split the air. Another contraction. Ruben guided Abby to hold the crowning head. Panting and then with determination the next contraction had Abby and Ruben holding a small slippery little bundle in a rush, and a lusty cry split the air.

Ruben stared at his crinkled face and stock of red hair glued to his head in a smear of birth water and blood. "This boy is certainly his father's son," he declared as he enveloped his body in white linen. "I swear this little mite, is a small Ted, wrapped in a petticoat."

He handed him to Callie, and she burst into tears. "Oh! My Theodore is adorable!" she sobbed. They improvised with twisted rag to tie the cord and used Ruben's pocketknife to cut it. They cleaned up and dealt with the last remaining birthing matters, they padded more folded petticoat to absorb the birthing loss. Callie put little Theodore to the breast and smiled through her tears and grimaces as after-birth contractions came hard and strong while he suckled.

Abby sat back on her haunches against the slabbed timber wall, looked to the rafters and took some deep rasping breaths. Tears tracked through her exhaustion. Babies being born in sheds: that really should not be a trend, regardless of what Ruben suggested. Childbirth was not at all as gentle or as beautiful or as ethereal as she had been taught was a woman's maternal duty. Madonna and child were as earthy, and as difficult, and as real, as giving birth in a shed, with hay, and pain, and the isolation of not having someone with you who knows what they are doing.

It seemed impossible that they had got through it and Callie was safe. Soon a midwife would check little Theodore over to give him a tick of approval. But even as Abby watched Callie snuggle her baby at her breast, she felt confident they would be okay.

⁂

Wilson rode up with three troopers. Ruben smiled and ran his hand through his hair, the tension releasing across his shoulders. "Wilson! Now the cavalry arrives, when all the hard work is done! One felon apprehended, one baby delivered, and four abducted hostages set free."

They dismounted quickly and arrested Pittman, pulling him to his feet. Their officious manner could not dampen Ruben's exhilaration in this moment. Abby and the other women were safe; a little life had been ushered into the world; his mother was smiling, the pain of her labour forgotten. Justice was being served. With Pittman apprehended they could now discover the quarter who had hired his services. He spoke to the troopers as they came over to him. "Mrs Horne has just given birth. She and the child are safe, but having a midwife check her and the baby must be a priority. I rode over to Redwood before, and they are bringing some transport so the ladies can make their way home."

They turned to him, ignoring Ruben's hand reached out in greeting. "Mr Ruben Davey," said the first, "You are under arrest for the abduction and unlawful detention of Mrs Abigail Bates, Mrs Callie Horne, Mrs Francine Moore, and Miss Caroline Winnicott." They cuffed him roughly as a horse drawn paddy-wagon appeared and both prisoners were taken away.

⁂

22

Abby entered the Courtroom, not as the mourning Widow Bates, nor as the respectable and eye-catching Abigail, but as poor unfortunate Bee. She sat beside Callie who was rocking her toddler Theodore, snuggled in sleep against her shoulder. Bee looked around. The men from the firm sat stern and severe. The women who once tittered over her teacups were silent and scandalized. The men in the jury box shuffled their feet restlessly, wondering if the trial would be drawn out and tiresome, because they had more pressing engagements to give their time and attention to.

"All rise! The honourable Judge Hanaway presiding."

It had been determined that Ruben intended to deviate from normal protocol to represent himself during the proceedings. Hanaway sat in a flurry of gown, raised his brow, adjusted his wig, and leaked a smile, suggesting that he anticipated this morning was potentially more interesting than what a usual day of proceedings presented.

"State your name for the record."

"Ruben Edward Davey." He sat quiet and sure. His beard was shaved; his moustache trimmed; his collar pristine; his cravat tied expertly, and his coat pressed. He didn't look like one who was fighting for his life, but Ruben knew the truth of it.

"Do you swear on this Holy Bible to tell the truth, the whole truth and nothing but the truth, so help you God?"

He so swore. Declaring God's Holy name over these events was a prayer on his heart.

On and on. The proceedings started to blur. The case against Ruben was being solidly constructed: his resentment against the firm; the circumstances of the embezzlement; the betrayal executed by Mrs

Bates and then her abduction; his access to the other hostages; the familiar territory where the hostages were held; his presence at the Shipman Downs' shed. He had motive, opportunity and there was physical evidence a plenty.

<hr>

Ruben stood. "Your Honour, I call Mr Patrick Pittman." He was sworn in. "Mr Pittman, do you live in the area known in Greystone as The Slum?"

"Yeah. So?"

"So, what do you do for a living, Mr Pittman?"

"A bit of this. A bit of that."

"A bit of what specifically, Mr Pittman?"

"Odd jobs."

"What was the nature of these odd jobs that finances your unusual level of comfort for a typical resident of Greystone's slums?"

"I chop wood. I fix hinges. I pasture the horses for the stable-hand at the livery yard... take them out to The Common."

"Did you ever chop wood or fix hinges for Constable Harold Wilson?"

"Only hinges he'd be needed fixin' would be the gaol house. I don't do gaol houses." There was a snigger around the room and the judge banged his gavel.

"What job did Constable Harold Wilson pay you for, if it wasn't fixing hinges?"

He scanned through the gallery intently, trying to locate the snitch. "I dunno. Pest control maybe." He smirked and showed a row of yellowed teeth, stained from the tobacco he smoked.

154

"For the record, the date was Wednesday, the seventeenth of March 1880. And can you tell the court what happened this night when you were abducted from your home?"

She shuffled her fan and adjusted her hat. "I was getting ready to retire, and I heard my little Dewy barking. My husband was out for the night, so I didn't expect him home until late. I went out to the living room to settle Dewy, and I was grabbed from behind."

"Did you see who grabbed you?" he asked in quiet horror.

"No, it was dark, and he was behind me. It was terrible! I was all alone!"

"That must have been terrifying for you, Mrs Moore. Was it usual for you to be all alone, while your husband was away on a Wednesday night?"

"Well only sometimes... when he has occasions or work meetings. It is not a regular thing if that is what you are meaning. But usually there is a servant or two. I always have someone around. But this night the servants were off because it was St Patrick's Day. They were happy about the Irish thing. I thought it was unnecessary. The men grabbed me with their filthy hands; and gagged me with disgusting rags; and dumped me on the back of a putrid cart all tied up." She shuddered in revulsion.

"Mrs Moore, you have my sympathies. Can you please read this note that I submit into evidence?"

She frowned as she stared at it. "It says: '*As arranged, Wed 17: 8*'."

"What does it refer to?"

The furrow of her frown deepened. "I don't know. It seems like details of an appointment or a meeting."

"Well, this year, the only month where the seventeenth falls on a Wednesday is in March. This is the day you stated you were abducted from your home."

"Well, like I said, my husband had a meeting at the club – he left to be there at six o'clock so it could refer to that."

"Who is it addressed to?"

"It doesn't say".

"Whose hand is it written in?"

"It looks like my husband's script…"

"His name, Mrs Moore?"

"It looks like the writing of my husband, Mr Herbert Moore."

"You are familiar with your husband's associates. Can you enlighten us to who may need this information, someone who wouldn't have normal access to published events? Was someone away?"

"I have no idea. The men keep the club business to themselves. It doesn't make sense."

"But you have confirmed this is your husband's handwriting, sharing this information, which is the exact day, date, and time of your abduction? Which would mean, whoever received this intelligence, knew that you would be left alone at home on this Wednesday evening?"

"That's ridiculous! Herbert would never jeopardise his family. I am his wife." But even as she said it, a cloud of doubt was gathering like a storm on her brow.

※

"I call Miss Caroline Winnicott to the stand."

"What is the nature of your relationship with Constable Harold Wilson, Miss Winnicott?"

"We are keeping company. It is our hope that we will soon be able to formally announce our betrothal."

"Soon? Is something holding you back?"

"Well, not myself. Or Harold, of course. My father did have some reservations, but that has been resolved now."

"Mr Winnicott had some reservations regarding your preferred intended? Did your father tell you the nature of his reservations, Miss Winnicott?"

She looked around and swallowed. "He did not think Harold had sufficient standing... in the community. I thought the profile he had acquired in the Inland Ambush arrests was a positive thing, but recently, my father disclosed that he did not like Harold's involvement. He said that was an inappropriate controversy for a Winnicott. He felt Harold was not the type of son-in-law worthy of a merchant empire. That sort of thing."

"We have heard a witness say that your father told him that he thought Harold Wilson was *"a powerless, unimpressive sort of suitor"*. That is a harsh summation of the man courting the daughter of Mr Bertrand Winnicott, of Winnicott Textiles Importers and Suppliers. This is the man that you love."

"Well, yes. But Harold is not like that at all. And Father can be... inflexible. Harold was troubled that my father didn't respect him as my intended. But he told me he would win him over."

"Did he have a plan to do that?"

"He was very confident that he would be able to persuade my father that he was ambitious and could provide for me in a suitable manner."

"Did he disclose the basis of this confidence?"

"He didn't say. But it didn't matter in the end, because when I was abducted, I knew that Harold would come through. Harold found me and brought me home. His name has indeed been vindicated. As one receiving esteemed community recognition of a local hero, my father no longer has reason to resist our relationship. My father has already told me he will offer us his blessing to be married and he has even nominated an allowance after our nuptials."

"So, since your abduction, and subsequent rescue, your father's reservations about your relationship have been allayed, and now your father has in fact offered you an allowance to start married life?"

"Well, of course. Harold rescued me. I am his only daughter. It is not remarkable that his valour would be so rewarded."

"Hmm. That's a lot of motive, Miss Winnicott."

"What are you suggesting?" Ruben stood still and tilted his head slightly. She gasped and went bright red, flushing in anger. "No! How dare you! He would *never*! Harold loves me!"

"Very much, it would seem, Miss Winnicott. Enough to marry."

❧❧❧❧❧

"I call Mrs Callie Horne to the stand. Mrs Horne, what happened during the time you were interned at the Shipman Downs' barn?"

"I went into labour, and I gave birth to my son."

"Were you afraid, Mrs Horne, that this might be dangerous to you or your baby?"

"I wasn't to start with, but Mistress Abby was very distressed. She was afraid something might go wrong, and we wouldn't be able to get help in time."

"Can you point out your son so that we can see he is here with you?"

"Yes Sir. Over there. That is my Theodore."

"He seems a robust, healthy little lad. How old is he now?

"He is just on one year old."

"And what did you name him?"

"Theodore Jacob Ruben Horne. Theodore after my husband Ted, Jacob is a family name – after my father and brother, and Ruben – after you, Sir."

"But I am being accused of abducting you. Why would you name your son after someone who put your life in danger?"

"Oh, Sir! That is ridiculous! Of course, I would never name my child after a kidnapper. You didn't abduct us. You found us and saved us. You know you did. You even rode over to Redwood Park for help. And when you came back, Mistress Abby was more settled, because you were right there helping us through it."

"So just to be clear: you named your son after someone who helped you. You assert I did not abduct you, or jeopardise you and your baby's life in anyway?"

"Oh, Sir, you saved our lives. You know it. The police came along well after you found us and after little Theodore was born. You didn't even run when they got there."

⁂

"I call Miss Bee... umm... Miss Bee Hives to the stand." Bee stood up and shuffled to the witness stand.

"State your name for the record."

"Mrs Abigail Bates," she mumbled with her head bowed.

Ruben looked around the courtroom. No one was interested in the vagabond witness. "Pardon me Ma'am. Can you speak up? Your name please, for the record?"

She sat up straight. "Mrs Abigail Bates," she stated clearly, looking directly at Ruben. There were gasps from the women in the gallery. Surely not! They leant forward staring at her, curiously scandalised. Perhaps this actually was her! Had the beautiful widow fallen so far, in just over a year? Who knew she had been here in the courtroom all along? No wonder she presented with a false name.

"But you came forward when I called Miss Bee Hives to the stand."

"It is a pseudonym I use; Miss Bee is a character I play."

"Why would you do that?"

"Because I did not want to draw attention to myself. I was trying to stay in invisible, to blend into the Greystone neighbourhood."

"Why did you feel you needed to stay undetected Mrs Bates?"

"Because you told me that if people knew we were betrothed to be married it could jeopardise my safety and yours."

The courtroom erupted again. Ruben was satisfied. Attention was back on track. "Let the record show that Mrs Abigail Bates says she is betrothed – to myself, the disgraced lawyer accused of misappropriating funds from his previous employer and kidnapping herself and three other women. Why would you attach yourself to someone so shamed, Mrs Bates?"

"Because those accusations and the gossip connected with it, is not based on the true nature of who you are. I have only found you to be honest and straightforward."

"Objection your Honour. Given the betrothal, spousal privilege should apply. Mrs Bates is therefore not competent to testify."

"Just declaring the nature of this relationship your honour. We are not yet husband and wife, so spousal privilege cannot be claimed." The Judge permitted it, more out of amusement than the technicality. "Were you ever abducted by me, Mrs Bates, against your will?"

"No."

"How can that be, when there are a number of witnesses who say they saw you taken?"

"I was threatened, because I challenged the men on their refusal to pay the agreement we made. Their attitude turned belligerent, so you took me to safety."

"Hmm. You are referring to the agreement you made with the firm: Crosby and Moore, to provide information on my habits according to this advertised flyer. Were you ever paid for your service?"

"Not all of it. Only a small surety. They searched my belongings and said there was no evidence of such an agreement. They refused to pay on what was agreed."

"Your honour, I submit into evidence the said agreement signed by Mrs Bates, Mr Herbert Moore, and Mr Alfred Crosby, both partners in the said firm."

"Objection Your Honour. The detail of a back-yard agreement made so long ago can hardly be relevant to the matters at hand."

"This whole affair is back-yard. Signatures and financial commitments provide evidence of a pattern of business practice, Your Honour. It appears this contractual agreement was signed by both of the company's *partners*, and still, they ignore the obligation. Here are the names of five other businesses who claim the same disregard experienced in their dealings with this firm."

"Your Honour! Objection."

"Your Honour, the pattern demonstrated is that professional ethics weigh little into the way this firm makes decisions."

"I'll allow it." Again. Amused.

"Tell me Mrs Bates, what did you learn when you disguised yourself as Miss Bee Hives."

"I learnt that children who live in the Greystone neighbourhood have little food and no school. I learnt the living conditions and sanitation of the homes are primitive and the people there live in squalor. I learnt that Constable Wilson had been regularly passing money to Mr Pittman. The local opinion is that Pittman does unsavoury jobs that..."

"Objection! Hearsay Your Honour."

"I saw Constable Wilson give money to Pittman twice. Both people were clearly visible."

"Your Honour, conjecture. There is no evidence that money was exchanged. Their conversation could have been about anything, such as offering directions in an unfamiliar part of town."

"One does not usually count directions."

"Noted." Ruben nodded and paused. "Mrs Bates, when was Miss Bee kidnapped?"

"It was not my character Bee who was kidnapped. But myself: Mrs Abigail Bates. I was taken from my home early hours of Thursday morning." Bee took a washer and began to remove her make up.

There were gasps of shock and scandalous frowns, and more wagging of feathered fans. "Objection Your Honour, this theatrical farce is making a mockery of your courtroom!"

"Your honour, when she took the stand, she identified as Mrs Abigail Bates, not this poor fictitious persona. It seems she will be taken more seriously if she stands before the court as herself. It was expedient to demonstrate how convincing her disguise was, so that it is understood how she witnessed these events unobserved by the parties concerned."

"Objection. If she felt she would not be taken seriously, she should have thought about that when she got dressed this morning!" The exclamations of shock proceeded to escalate.

"Order in the Court! You may proceed, Mrs Bates."

Abby took off her hat, and her hair was arranged tidily underneath. She peeled off her tatted oversized dress and pinafore, revealing a fitted sober day-dress underneath. Soon she was sitting demurely and tastefully as Mrs Abigail Bates. The gasps in the courtroom barely paused.

"Mrs Bates, did you see your captors?"

"Only one, and only once. That was when he brought Caroline Winnicott, bound, to the barn on Shipman Downs where we were held."

"Wasn't that at night, in the dark? How could you recognise your gaoler?"

"He carried a lamp and I saw his face in the light. I recognised the scar – on his left cheek. It was Mr Pittman, the man I witnessed receiving money from Constable Wilson... twice."

"Did Constable Wilson ever disclose he was courting the daughter of Mr Bertrand Winnicott, of Winnicott Textiles Importers and Suppliers?"

"No, he just told me the father of his lady-friend was a humble shop-owner, who valued a level of financial security for his daughter. It was Caroline Winnicott who told me her fiancé was in fact Harold Wilson."

"Did Miss Caroline Winnicott give you any indication that she was involved in her own abduction?"

"No, not at all. She appeared as confused and distressed as the rest of us. I suppose that since you had already been accused of kidnapping me, it seemed a logical course to continue building on that allegation."

"Your Honour. This is outrageous! Speculation!"

"The jury will disregard."

"How would Harold Wilson even know where you reside, when you had gone to so much trouble to remain anonymous?"

"He came to lunch at your invitation. He had become a trusted friend who told you he was supporting the investigation to vindicate your reputation."

⁓⁓⁕⁓⁓

"I call Sargent Jessup to the stand."

"Was Constable Harold Wilson ever commissioned to work undercover in a plain-clothes capacity?"

"No."

Can you offer a professional explanation of the exchanges that were described by witnesses?"

"No. I cannot explain how it relates to his duties in law-enforcement."

"What was the nature of the evidence that you found when you searched the domicile of Constable Harold Wilson?"

"We found a diary with meeting dates marked that correspond with witness accounts of the transactions previously discussed with Mr Pittman. There were entries of meetings that match your own diary: Ruben Davey. We found the note with the date you've submitted, in a waste bin. We found documents that have been identified as your investigation notes. These match the inventory of items taken from Mrs Bates residential unit. And we found a canvas bag containing bank notes under his floorboards. There were also bank transfers, and some bonds in the ceiling. This inventory shows that the amounts are large. The totals amount to more than the funds and items reportedly embezzled from the legal firm, Crosby and Moore. And there were other documents: letters of agreement, stating the terms of payment for 'services rendered' from that firm and other people."

"Did you find any corresponding evidence at the offices of Crosby and Moore?"

"There were a number of items of correspondence submitted as evidence. Of particular note is one letter to Mrs Bates, telling her to drop her requests for payment on the contract written up for reward for information, as they said there was no evidence such an agreement existed. Another was a letter written to Mr Harold Wilson dated the week of Mrs Moore's abduction. It is not clear what 'services rendered' refers to."

⚜

"Mr Herbert Moore, what was the nature of your agreement with Constable Wilson? What services were rendered?"

He sat in grim, stony silence. He would not allow his firm to be embroiled in this madness. Ruben quietly pushed him to answer. "You despicable filth!" he snapped. "You do not get to question me!"

"You are a man of the law, Mr Moore. You understand the need for your statement for the official record." Ruben waited and then repeated the question again.

The judge directed him to answer, and he sighed, and narrowed his eyes just a little. How could he contain the mess from all this mudslinging? "I was co-operating fully with Constable Wilson's investigations. My wife went missing and I was frantic with fear." He said that in a flat monotone. Mrs Francine Moore wriggled uncomfortably; her doting husband's attentions seemed less than convincing.

"I refer again to this note submitted into evidence. Can you confirm your wife's testimony? Whose hand is it written in?"

"I have no idea."

"Perhaps comparing to your diary, Mr Moore, may assist. You have a distinct hand. It hardly needs expert opinion, although I did seek that. Their report suggests forgery is unlikely."

He cleared his throat. "Very well. That is my handwriting."

"Why did you share this information, that corresponds to the exact day, date and time of your wife's abduction?"

Francine Moore started whimpering in the gallery. Those around her were fanning her face frantically. By the time he spoke she was gasping and sobbing hysterically. A lady-friend assisted her to her feet and led her down the stairs. The echo of the stairwell reverberated around the courtroom. "I am betrayed! For thirty pieces of silver! Less! He betrayed me for a gentleman's agreement and a box of cigars. My life is ruined! Ruined!"

"The accusation is absurd. Ridiculous. My wife has already stated I would never jeopardise my family."

"I have made no allegation regarding the care of your family. It is expected that harm was never intended. But rather, was not your participation part of a complicated ruse to frame another party?"

"The evidence only points to you. You will not get away with this."

"But this is your letter, written in your handwriting, found in Constable Wilson's domicile. That means that others are involved. It means *you* are involved."

"That is outrageous. What could I have to gain?"

"Exactly my question. Why was it urgent that you would work so diligently to have my professional credibility smeared so thoroughly? I submit these additional documents, including this ledger of correspondence, that was received after the Outback Ambush ruling was handed down. It shows that a significant sector of disenchanted clientele withdrew services from the firm of Crosby and Moore. Of course, it is entirely a person's right to choose whichever lawyers they please, but an exodus of this scale means that there was strong financial incentive to have me disbarred; to try and reclaim some of that offended clientele's business."

Moore's face reddened in rage. "You have no right! You ignorant upstart! Your legal expertise has no respect for cultural convention. This was for the greater good. We have an obligation to uphold an appropriate standard of social order."

"Fortunately for me, Mr Moore, the British Court rules on matters of law, and not on social whims and morés. The judgments of previous cases cannot be overturned, regardless of the blackening of my name. The Law of the British Empire stands above my reputation."

"This was just to expose who you really are! Wilson approached us. He insisted his initiative could not fail to point to yourself as the culprit!"

"And yet here you are on the stand, openly testifying that you had to generate fabricated evidence of my involvement, because it does not exist in reality. And although you intended no harm to befall your wife, such an internment was traumatising for all involved; a pregnant mother was put at risk; a newborn baby birthed in primitive and unsanitary circumstances. It amounts to Reckless Endangerment."

He growled low like a menacing dog. "To see you go down was worth every penny of the outlay."

"Although I am curious as to the intensity of your hate for me, Mr Moore, your motivation is not on trial here today; only that you conspired with Constable Wilson in perverting the course of justice; that you and your partners habitually set aside professional agreements for financial advantage; you participated in criminal acts of misappropriating funds, abduction, detaining a person without consent for advantage, and reckless endangerment; and that you would have my head on the block in your stead.

Nothing further, Your Honour."

⁕

Epilogue

They rode on horseback up into the hills. Abby looked at this landscape with new eyes of appreciation. She moved in closer to Ruben in the saddle. It felt like she was being lifted up into the clouds. When they arrived at camp the men stood formally for their captain as he dismounted and assisted Abby down. Abby smiled and gave Callie a warm hug standing beside Ted, holding their son close in her arms.

There was a lamb roasting on the fire, and Abby looked at it suspiciously. Dickens cleared his throat and spoke up. "Cook. She donated some things... for her mistress's wedding."

"But I am no longer her Mistress..."

Cook stepped forward. "I covered it with Gillis Ma'am. No theft has been committed."

"Cook! You are here! This is indeed a wonderful surprise!" Abby exclaimed. Hawk grunted and Dickens beamed.

Ruben looked around at everyone. "Today has been a long time in the making... it is a day of celebration! May I present to you my wife: Mrs Abigail Davey. Let's eat and enjoy the good company and great food." He said a blessing, and the men filled up an assortment of chipped pannikins, mugs, and tumblers with ale from the barrel that had found its way to their camp from the Homestead cellar. Abby smiled delightedly. All the fine crystal of a thousand estates could not compare with the excellence of this banquet. They made a toast to the Bride and Groom, and then tucked into the feast held in their own glorious reception-hall. A table with two chairs was set overlooking the spectacular views of the valley. Ruben gallantly assisted Abby to her seat and pushed in her chair. "I once promised you Afternoon Tea from my balcony overlooking spectacular views," he said.

Abby smiled. "You have not disappointed. Quite an impressive setting for a wedding supper."

Cook served their meal, while the men hung around the campfire on various stumps and logs and rocks. Someone produced a banjo. It was an out-of-tune sort of affair, but it didn't stop them from singing and sharing jokes and the party proceeded. When they had finished eating, Ruben made a speech and spoke with a couple of men as they continued helping themselves to second and third helpings.

Abby asked Jay about the condition of his arm. He raised his brow and grinned around some of Cook's roasted rib bones. He licked his fingers dripping with Hawks' "special" gravy, so designated because of the cheap wine and generous number of lumps that bulked out the sauce. Jay tossed the bones into the fire, wiped his hands across his trousers and then stripped off his shirt to bare his scars. He rolled his shoulder and flexed his arm with pride. "You were right, Ma'am. It has a good yarn attached to it. I'm still working on getting it strong." And he picked up a piece of wood to demonstrate his progress.

"I'm glad it is coming on."

That was license for Ted to take off his shirt and show his back criss-crossed with fading marks of scar tissue. Another downed his drink and bared a scar on his side, sharing his even larger story. And so, the party went on. Someone ribbed Dickens on not having a wound to uncover. He shrugged, and someone else jibed, "He can't rip open his chest to parade a broken heart."

Another raised his mug. "It's Cook, ain't it? She's poisoned your good sense with her food. You were a goner with that very first loaf of bread that Mistress Abby sent up here!" And they joked and rollicked and stoked the fire with their fun. He growled and sat away from the others.

Cook bashfully plied Dickens with another serve of dessert pie and sat beside him on the log, to check everything was to his satisfaction. He smiled and blushed and tucked in; taking a swig of ale every now and then, to find the right amount of courage to talk.

Ruben quietly eased Abby away from the noise. They watched the valley wash with golden light as the horizon tinged in halos of deep colour lighting the clouds with fiery reds, oranges, and deep purple from the setting sun.

As dusk faded, he lifted the canvas door to his cave, "Come back in here..." and led her inside. She blushed at the audience that was still hooting and joking around the fire. "We can outwait them, but they will respect our privacy. No fear."

She felt sort of dazed. She walked around touching his stuff. She traced his initials carved in his desktop. "Ahh, Captain R.E.D. Mr Ruben Edward Davey. You were right when you said your men lacked imagination in devising pseudonyms and nicknames."

"What they lack in imagination, they make up for in loyalty."

Everything was as it used to be... crude and rough and improvised. Yet it was a wonderful, adventurous, protected, clean sort of 'rough'. And this time there was a double bed... covered in a comforter that was not so ascetic.

Ruben stood watching her with a satisfied grin and lit the cracked lamp to light up the shadows. "The first time I saw you here, Mistress Abby, you made quite an impression."

"You accused me of being independent, subversive, and rebellious."

"That I did. Perhaps there still a little truth in this, Mrs Davey. It surely applies... for you to even contemplate being here now."

"If you only knew how much you changed my world. It was like I had jumped into the cold waters of a billabong... and it took my breath away. I had imagined love like that, but I never imagined it was so close."

"It was so close and yet so far away." He turned around and his serious green eyes held the sting of remorse. "Abby... please forgive me if loving you somehow caused you to sin..." He shook his head. He could not really understand how he could have done it any differently. He hadn't pursued her; he hadn't intended to feel such intensity; he had never acted on it ... and yet he was still haunted by the idea that perhaps he had he crossed the line into adultery and caused her to do the same. The idea was a cloud of shame over their marriage.

"You know Ruben, I was also tormented by that accusation. I never told anyone of Sorenson's abuses because I knew they would tell me it was my duty as a wife to take the hard with the soft. You helped me see I could be safe... that I *needed* to be safe. After I brought you those rations from the Shearer's Feast, I decided to leave Sorensen. The idea of escaping him... in my heart, I felt God would endorse me doing what I needed to do to be safe. I had reconciled myself to the reality that I could never obtain a certificate of divorce because Sorenson was so respected in the community. I had settled within myself that all my life I would remain married until death parted us. I decided I could do nothing about that, but I could escape and disappear. That I would do. I was working on a plan, formulating the details on how and when. I would have done it except for his stroke."

Ruben took her in his arms. "Abby... my anger at the Shearer's Feast... I didn't want to admit it was not just about my men. But if I could not have you... I would want you safe."

"But Ruben, you said something in the courtroom that helped me. You said to Mr Moore that it was not the intensity of his emotion that was on trial; only what he did and how he had participated in these things. It was his actions that he was judged on. I cannot believe that the law of God... and his justice, could be any different. What I mean is our feelings are not on trial. It is not that we felt so intensely that becomes adultery, but we are held to account with what we did with those feelings..."

"But Jesus said... if we think in our heart..."

"Can you not see a distinction between what I feel and what I think? I felt. Oh, I felt! But what I thought... my only thought was to honour God and to navigate this situation in the best way I could. Ruben, you had that same sense of honour. I am grateful... so grateful, that you never pursued me... because if you had, I am quite sure I would not have had the strength or the will, not to respond. For that I am so very grateful. It means we start now without that shadow of adultery over our marriage."

He tilted his head... and felt a weight lift from his chest. "You are a wise woman, Abigail Davey. We have traversed some difficult terrain since that first time you arrived here uninvited, and yet somehow, we are back here now, and you are loving me still."

Abby walked back into the recesses of the cave. "When I felt I couldn't go on I would imagine myself here... as one of your men, sleeping in the alcoves of this cave. I felt so protected. Safe."

He grinned and came over to her, tucking a strand of her fair hair back behind her ear. "Believe me, I have no interest in you being one of my men. It is so much more appealing that you are my wife."

"Being safe... feeling safe... that has been so foreign to me. I resented that I had no idea what it was like to live in peace at Redwood Park. But now you offer me peace, but I believe there is still much more to come. All of this is beyond my most extravagant expectations."

"Perhaps we could amend the meaning of your name to be, '*My husband is joyful.*' I don't think it would be an exaggeration."

"Is it possible that I am walking out on the other side of *Meantime* now... with a taste of joy on my lips?" she said with a beautiful smile.

He smiled. "Perhaps I could check?" and he kissed her lips lightly. "Hmm. Yes... that has the taste of joy. I thought it was a most unusual request to have these mountains as a honeymoon destination."

"I guess I wanted to acknowledge that this cave has represented our Meantime... and even if this is what it looks like until the end of time... then I will be content. It has been our time of grace, even if it means, I never hold any 'lavish comforts' again, I would still make the same choice and travel with you through this place in a heartbeat." And she reached up and caressed his face and drew him further into the cool recesses of the cave with a kiss.

⁂

The men dispersed, leaving the honeymooning couple alone. Ruben woke to the fresh smell of mountain mist. He leant up on his elbow watching his wife sleep beside him. Her eyelids fluttered open, and he thought his heart would melt from the fire he felt as he kissed her good morning.

176

"Perhaps now would be a good time to tell you..." he smiled through his kisses.

"Tell me what?"

"I have been given an invitation to sit on an advisory board as legal counsel... to the Governor."

She blinked away the echoes of a dream, and sat up. "Oh? Such an invitation sounds very respectable."

"It is very respectable, Mrs Davey. Why do you sound doubtful?"

"My heart was stolen by a bushranger, and I am not sure it has been recovered yet. I would not have thought grand-larceny would be respectable enough for such illustrious company."

"The governor said he has been tracking my work, particularly in how I advocated on various cases. He was waiting for my clearance to practice again before he approached me. Oh, and on the matter of the cardiac grand-larceny, I have that heart carefully in my custody. But other than that: I am finished storming fortresses to liberate fair maidens from their captors."

"And yet I was being quite serious. Advisory sounds clean, but will it be enough for you, Ruben? I have noticed you seem unable to resist diving in close and getting your hands dirty."

"I have given sober consideration to how to add weight to this offer, to make it more than a sanitised advisory role. I understand the risk of this ending up a useless paper tiger without teeth to accomplish anything practically worthwhile. I submitted a counter-proposal to address that."

"So, my serious husband... what practical worthwhile counter-proposal did you suggest?"

"Advisory yes, but overseeing specific commissions to address reforms around a cluster of target projects: schools for the Jimmy's and the Mildred's; medical clinics for the Teds and Jays; maternal care for the Callie's; small business support for the Hawks and Dickens. I am going to pursue that contract that the firm has not honoured and use the money as the basis for a loan trust for seeding small businesses. I've been given a commitment that he will at least deliberate on my proposal."

"That is quite an eclectic list of reforms."

"I thought you may have considered there was something I had missed."

"Like...?"

"Like... I was thinking that list might include a home for my wife and my children, without the sewer rats or the need to dress-down to go out."

She laughed and brushed his face. "That is part of the *Meantime* that I will not miss. I think I could allow you to advise me on that."

"Advise you? You take on the function of Governor in our home?"

"I prefer to think of it as advising each other. Side by side... in the Meantime, until we reach the destination," she smiled gently.

"But what if we never arrive? What if we are in this, side-by-side... working towards whatever next adventure that comes across our path, leading to the next," he said.

"Perhaps you are on to something. The 'Meantime' always seemed to be an unwanted place to me: a place to tolerate or escape. But this? This idea of Time together is much more appealing. I am very content to be with you Ruben, side-by-side, in this Time. Forever-now."

Coming soon from Olwyn Harris: Pioneers of Grace Series

Book 2 - Circle of Grace

All her life Hannah had been sensible and sincere. When her humble circumstances lead her to work as the companion for Lady Whitmore, she is confronted with Lady Whitmore's nephew, the most shallow and irresponsible man she has ever met. As their life of privilege collapses around them, will she follow Lady Whitmore and Sebastian to Australia, to explore a new life in exile?

Book 3 - Journey of Grace

Tibby had grand dreams that were very different from the squalor of the textile mill tenements where she grew up. She plotted her escape by taking sponsored passage to the Colony as a bride, but everything on this journey was harder than even she could imagine. Dumped like garbage at the gate of Zachary Logan's place, will it be possible for Tabitha to sew a new life together in this barren wasteland of Australia?

Book 4 - Mask of Grace

Late one night, Martha finds herself at a wayside inn, running from the expectations of her family. To stay in hiding, she works as a scullery maid alongside Simmons, who doesn't just cook, but is a culinary artist. Intrigued by each other's secrets, will they be able to drop their pretence long enough to find their true passions?

Book 5 – Crucible of Grace

Ruth has had more than her fair share of tragedy. When her widowed mother-in-law wants to return to the farming region where her family once thrived, Ruth works as a laundry maid to support them. Can Ruth survive the fire of heartache and prejudice to find a new shape for her life, which might even include the station owner?

Book 6 – Sculpture of Grace

Rachel loves her country life. She loves her art of forging iron and her growing friendship with the station's newest blacksmith. Leah, her older sister, on the other hand, does not like anything country. But, as fate would have it, Rachel is offered a proposal which means she would have to leave the valley she loves, while Leah is sidelined and mourns her dreams of more. Can the sisters find a way to reconcile their destinies and forge a different story where they both see their dreams come true?

More Books by this Author
Stand-alone Stories

Matt's Boys of Wattle Creek

When Matthew Lawson's three sons were born, he wrote each of them a letter outlining his hopes and prayers for their futures. When he decided to give up his city job and move to the little town of Wattle Creek, he could never have imagined the effect it would have on his young family. As Matt's boys grow to maturity and find their places in their community, will his dreams and prayers come to fulfilment? Will his boys develop their own faith in the eternal God? And will they each find the kind of love that Matt holds for his beautiful Josie?

Maggie & Minotaur

"For Maggie, the mythical Minotaur represented Romance – half man, half beast. The Minotaur was a monster created from centuries of classical Greek mythology and no normal man could withstand its strength...... Sooner or later she would accept that Theseus, the hero, did not exist. She knew that she would have to battle through the maze of reality and confront it herself...." Maggie Wick was shipped off to the city and high society life at the age of 12, where she would learn the ways of the rich and marry into a family of influence. What could have caused her sudden return to Henderson's Gap? Can she really settle back into life on the station, with all its diversity and challenges? Will she find fulfilment in her role as provisional schoolteacher? Will she ever figure out the "Captain", the mysterious, intimidating, station manager? When war comes to her little haven and Maggie's world comes crashing down, taking her loved ones and the captain with it, Maggie needs to find a way to survive. Will her faith be enough to protect her, and what of the Captain? Could he really be the Theseus who would do battle with her Minotaur?

#1 The Beachside Cottage

In this offering from Olwyn Harris, we meet the heartbroken and downtrodden Eliza-Beth Perkins. Eliza-Beth is facing the dire consequences of her choices and the possibility of life in the poorhouse. Then she, literally, runs into Jensen Harker. Jensen is facing his own heartbreak at the death of his wife and wants nothing more than to be left alone. But something in Eliza-Beth stirs him to make a rash proposal, thus rescuing her from her predicament. As we follow their journey together, will we see them find the healing they both desperately need?

#2 Petrea Downs

In the 2nd book in this series, we meet Meg. Meg's life has been turned upside-down, with her husband gone, trying to run Petrea Downs by herself, and disaster after disaster at every turn. Thankfully, her neighbour Everett Grossman is always there to help. The final blow comes when a cattle duffer tries to steal her only source of income, gets shot, and has to be nursed back to health in her living room. But, is Ben Harker really the villain he seems? And is Everett really the hero he makes himself out to be?

#3 The Writer's Retreat

The third book in the Homes of Healing trilogy introduces us to Tess, a romance writer, who prides herself on letting her characters tell their own story. When she arrives at Rocky Creek B&B, the run-down stone cottage looks like the perfect place for her to retreat to, not only to write her book, but to escape her past. Join her as she discovers her characters and explores their stories and finds that God is intent on becoming part of her own story at the same time. As her relationship with the local publican challenges her to stop running, she realises that real life and real love can be messy and complicated. Can she honestly confront the ugly aspects in her own story, so that God can bring them both to a place of healing?

#1 Sapphires of Hope

"There is no way," she thought, "that I am going to use this!" She had desperately searched their cupboards for something, anything that would come close to what she needed for her catering project. She found only this old, dilapidated breadbasket that looked like the sort of junk that comes from one of those tacky jumble-sale stalls..."

Andi and Jo are best friends... they do pretty much everything together. So, when Andi has a catering assignment due, and only a tacky old basket to use, Jo helps her pull off the faded decorations, revealing a time-capsule of historical information, and in order to understand what it means, Andi and Jo ask their elderly neighbour to take them to visit the farm where the basket came from. They find themselves dumped back in history at the time of Federation, embroiled in circumstances that nearly cost Andi her life and threatens the livelihood of the people living there. How can they ever hope to keep going when things are spinning out of control?

#2 Rubies of Ambition

In the 2nd book in the Gem of Australia series, we again travel with Andi and Jo back in time. On this adventure, they meet the very beautiful and ambitious actress, Lillian Browning, who is on the run from the federal police. Andi and Jo accompany her back to her hometown, where they find she is not well received. Will Lillian find a balance between the past that calls her and the ambitions that drive her?

#3 Emerald Dreams

In the third instalment of the *Gems of Australia* series, Olwyn Harris brings Australian history to life as she takes us on a journey back to the early days of convict settlement in Australia. Here we, once again, find Andi and Jo learning about Australia's true history, and finding strength in God to help others.

#1: A Spacious Place

In this first instalment of the Guthrie's Lot series, set in the late 1800s, we meet Irvin Guthrie, a practical, no-nonsense man with a sick wife and a small child to care for. When his wife's doctor suggests they move to a warmer climate, he spends everything he has on a property that ends up not being what he expected. Joanna Grenham has dreams of being a schoolteacher. When an opportunity presents itself, she jumps at the chance, only to find herself given no choice but to care for Irvin's sick wife and child.

Will Irvin and Joanna make the most of their circumstances, or will they forever find life as hard and unyielding as the ground in A Spacious Place.

#2: A Level Path

In the second instalment of the Guthrie's Lot series, it is now the late 1960s. Here we meet Irvin's granddaughter Iris. Iris hungers for excitement and adventure, and she won't find that in Gumleigh, or with the ever-predictable Dave. The last thing she expected was for Dave to follow her across the world to England as she tries to find direction and meaning.

Will Iris finally see through the charismatic, but ultimately selfish, Stan, or will Dave leave England alone and leave Iris to find her own way to A Level Path?

#3: The Crying Tree

In this final episode of the Guthrie's Lot series, the year is now 2010. We meet Mac, who has always been an achiever – a do-er, just like her father. After the death of her mother, she finds that she needs to get away, so she buys a little run-down stone cottage in the middle of nowhere to transform into a creative studio. She is taken by the feel of the place - especially the twisted weeping willow tree behind the house, even though it doesn't fit into her plans anywhere.

Dan spent years growing up on the old Guthrie place, so when the new owner arrives, he is not convinced that he wants to work for this headstrong woman, who is obviously used to getting what she wants, but he feels that it is something he has to do – and only God knows why.

Can Dan and Mac work together to make her dreams into a reality? Will she transform the old Guthrie place, and her life, into something unique and beautiful? And what will become of Thy Crying Tree.

The Bush Olympics

The Bush Olympics, written by Olwyn Harris and beautifully illustrated by Shelly Askew, shows us that we don't have to be good at everything to be part of a team. Even sleepy Koala is good at something, and if everyone plays their part, we can all be successful together.

www.ingramcontent.com/pod-product-compliance
Lightning Source LLC
Chambersburg PA
CBHW070956180726
48291CB00004B/1324